THE
MOST
DANGEROUS
PROFESSION

Center Point
Large Print

Also by Clifton Adams and available from Center Point Large Print:

A Partnership with Death

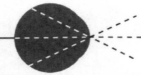

THE
MOST
DANGEROUS
PROFESSION

Clifton Adams

CENTER POINT LARGE PRINT
THORNDIKE, MAINE

This Center Point Large Print edition
is published in the year 2019 by arrangement with
Golden West Literary Agency.

Originally published in the US by Doubleday.
Originally published in the UK by Collins.

The text of this Large Print edition is unabridged.
In other aspects, this book may vary
from the original edition.
Printed in the United States of America
on permanent paper.
Set in 16-point Times New Roman type.

ISBN: 978-1-64358-374-7 (hardcover)
ISBN: 978-1-64358-378-5 (paperback)

The Library of Congress has cataloged this record under
Library of Congress Control Number: 2019945580

ONE

All that day the hard-eyed men had straggled down from Laredo and Hidalgo and a hundred other border crossings that the Mexicans were too busy to patrol. It was hot and their shabby, hodgepodge uniforms of butternut and gray were rimed with sweat. The chalky dust of Nuevo Leon lay on their faces like death masks.

In their eyes was a dumb hostility that dared anyone to try to stop them. Somewhere in Monterrey, they had heard, members of Marshal Bazaine's staff were signing on recruits. That was where they were so determinedly headed.

This was a year of hate and anger—1865. These men had just lost one of the bloodiest wars in history and could not wait to sign on for another.

From his guard post on the outskirts of Monterrey, Legionnaire Second Class William Olive regarded the ragged procession with indifference. He had been in Mexico for two years. Before that he had survived Magenta and Solferino and had soldiered against Barbary pirates and Berber tribesmen. There was nothing left for him to learn about the brutality of war.

Legionnaire Olive found these defeated Confederates faintly ridiculous in their amateurish approach to war. He would have found them almost comic—if he had been interested enough to think about them at all. They took the loss of war so personally, made such a tragedy of defeat.

But he did not care about these men. He understood the need that drove these shabby leftovers of war from one inferno to another, but it was no affair of his. In Sidi-bel-Abbès they said, *A moi la Légion*! For the man who had nothing, there was always the profession of arms. *"The Legion is your country."* Your home. Your family. Your life. These ragged Confederates had learned that much, at least. When war was all a man knew, there was no place for him except an army. Any army.

Of course, as Legionnaire Olive knew, these Confederates had not had all the amateurishness knocked out of them yet. They still thought in terms of "causes," and they dreamed of the impossible, of reviving and salvaging a lost war.

All that would change, in time. They would learn that losing wars was the true job of the professional soldier; defeat was a thing that amateurs did not dirty themselves with. In time they too would become experts in the art of fighting for hopeless causes, or perhaps for no cause at all.

In that year of 1865 the French Foreign Legion was little more than thirty years old; its spiritual home was Africa, but legionnaires died, as was their job, in all parts of the world for two francs a month and the glory of France. At the moment First Company, Third Battalion, *Légion Etrangère*, found itself in Mexico. Two years ago they had left Sidi-bel-Abbès with the band playing, *Eugénie, les larmes aux yeux, nous venons te dire adieu*. With tears in their eyes they were bidding good-by to the Empress of France. If only the Empress could have heard the names they called her in Bel-Abbès!

The company had participated in the spring offensive, scattering Mexican armies and sending many of their officers fleeing across the border into the United States. Juárez, Olive had heard, was dead and it had begun to look as if the war was nearly over. But the United States did not fancy a European power so near its border. The French lines were painfully thin; under no condition could they risk provoking the huge Union Army which was still intact and battle-ready. Marshal Bazaine, an old legionnaire himself, had held the company at Monterrey.

Now, for several days disturbing news had filtered through from the south. Bazaine was in trouble. The Mexicans refused to accept Maximilian as their emperor, and Juárez was not dead. In truth, he was very much alive and was regrouping his armies for an effort which could sweep the French into the sea.

To the Legion it was an old story which would

be repeated over and over for a hundred years. After the cause, hopeless in the beginning, was irretrievably lost, legionnaires would go on fighting and dying.

Legionnaire Olive paused for a moment in his clockwork marching back and forth in front of a plank barrier which the Americans merely rode or walked around. Most of these Confederates were Texans; some of them were old enough to remember the Alamo, and hating Mexicans was a tradition with them. They regarded Olive's uniform with suspicion, the baggy trousers, the white kepi, the heavy greatcoat that legionnaires always wore, even in the furnace heat of African deserts.

Olive's orders were to let the Americans pass; Bazaine needed all the soldiers he could get. Most of them rode bony nags and plow horses, and a few had even walked the long stretch from Laredo. Olive had heard that Texans made first-class cavalrymen. The French generals would be glad to see them.

The Americans insisted on fighting as units, as they had fought in their own war. The French had no objections. If they wanted to believe that one day they would form the nucleus of a powerful new Confederate army, then let them believe it. No one knew better than the French that fools often make magnificent soldiers.

Legionnaire Olive shrugged to himself. His

indifference to the misery of others was complete.

Occasionally a particular face or the uniform of a general officer would stir his interest for a moment. But even generals, if there were enough of them, ceased to be a curiosity. The Confederate general Slaughter was said to be negotiating with Bazaine for the transfer of twenty-five thousand soldiers to Mexico. General Banks had already taken part in the attack on Cortinas at Matamoras. Generals, professional and political, were flocking to Mexico. Smith, Shelby, Walker, Terrell, Magruder, Stone . . . Legionnaire Olive was becoming bored with Confederate generals.

But occasionally a face would catch his interest momentarily. A face somehow different from the others, not a soldier's face. A face that would be a little too smooth, the eyes merely cunning instead of angry. Where is this man going? Olive would wonder. What is he up to? Is he a spy? An adventurer?

Such a face belonged to the man named Trent. Olive knew instinctively that this was no soldier, although he wore odds and ends of Confederate uniforms, as did the others. He sat a regulation Union saddle—but then most of the Confederate cavalry had outfitted itself with captured Union arms and equipment. It seemed to Legionnaire Olive that the man's horse was a little too well fed and cared for, as was the man himself.

Unconsciously, Olive paused in his monotonous

marching. The legionnaire's glance crossed with Trent's, and they seemed to recognize the same hunger in each other's face. Standing there before the barrier, Olive watched the well-fed man on his well-fed horse continue along the goat trail to Monterrey. Then, as he stared, somehow knowing that he would meet the man again, a certain iciness that he knew only too well entered Olive's blood-stream.

He quickly resumed his mechanical marching—but it was much too late for that. Too late to save himself, no matter what he did. He did not have to turn around to know that his unsoldierly gawking had been observed.

The Legion had been created on the theory that few Frenchmen would be such fools as to enlist in a unit especially designed for the outcasts and undesirables of the world. The theory had proved correct. The absence of French citizens in its ranks freed the Legion of many political pressures. Discipline, to the wearers of the white kepi, was of an unusual order. An offense that would go unnoticed in another army would mean three months in the penal battalion for a legionnaire.

The legionnaire rarely saw his officers. In the world of *La Légion* the *sous-officier*, the non-com, wielded awesome power. His decisions in matters of discipline were absolute. At Legion headquarters in Sidi-bel-Abbès, this was the first lesson the new recruit learned. For the five years of his enlistment it would be the most important lesson of his life.

Legionnaire Olive, onetime Liverpool dock worker, brawler and, according to British police records, murderer, walked his post with ramrod perfection. No legionnaire ever marched or about-faced with such angular precision, or maintained such an admirably blind stare or wooden expression. But it was all too late.

At the opposite end of the barrier stood the iron figure of Sergent-Chef Giuseppe Ciano, quietly watching as Olive approached him. He stood wide-legged in the dust. Big, powerful, indestructible. Sergent-Chef Ciano's smile widened. His many small teeth glistened like nailheads as Olive's progress brought him ever nearer.

Olive halted at the exact extreme of his post, the toes of his heavy boots not more than the thickness of a film of dust from the *sergent-chef*'s own immaculately polished footgear. He stared with absolute blindness. The *sergent-chef*'s breath, an invisible wall of garlic and wine, bridged the distance of two inches that separated the tip of Olive's nose from the point of Sergent-Chef Ciano's square chin. The eyes of the *sous-officier* were dark, glistening, waiting expectantly for some part of Olive's body or equipment to touch him, an impertinence for which a legionnaire might be flogged to unconsciousness.

Olive about-faced. His insides dropped sickeningly when he felt the tail of his buttoned-back greatcoat slap against the *sergent-chef*'s thigh. When he about-faced at the opposite end of the barrier, he saw the broad back of Sergent-Chef Ciano moving with the authority and power of a dreadnought toward the next guard post. It was a sight that Legionnaire Olive welcomed—however, he knew that memories of *sous-officiers* were as long as infinity. An hour, a month, a year from now, when Ciano was displeased with some matter outside his field of control, or perhaps for no reason at all, he would send for Olive and recall this moment to mind.

In the same way Legionnaire Olive would grimly brighten and polish a vision in his own mind, that of the slack, smooth face of the man called Trent.

Legionnaire Olive found little of Mexico to his liking. The wine was thin and acid. The beer, which he knew to be excellent, somehow turned stale and sour in the glass of a soldier of France. The Mexicans were thoroughly hostile, the Indians treacherous. More than one member of First Company had come to an inglorious end in Monterrey, clubbed down in the dark streets or stabbed in the kidney with a prostitute's silver-handled stiletto.

Olive longed for the rich, blood-red *pinard* and

the raucous bordellos of Algeria. But if he could have been in Algeria he knew that he would be wishing for the thick ales and heady gins of Liverpool. And women that you didn't have to inspect for lice before turning to matters of amour. Such was life in the Legion.

At the moment Legionnaire William Olive was discussing with two comrades the eternal and unsolvable puzzle of survival.

"Listen to me," Legionnaire Franz Haupt was saying in German. "We'll all be dead before the month is out. Bazaine will be swept into the sea. Then what will we do?"

"Another Camerone," said Legionnaire Leonardo Bello in Italian. "Only worse."

"What could be worse than Camerone?" Olive asked in Liverpool English.

"At Camerone it was sixty-two legionnaires against two thousand Mexicans," Bello said gloomily. "Here we are one company against the whole of Northern Mexico. And maybe the Union Army of the United States, as well."

"This is terrible beer," Haupt said. "I have heard that these Mexicans put dead rats in the beer they serve to legionnaires. I can believe it."

Bello spat on the dirt floor of the adobe cantina. "This wine is vinegar, and bad vinegar at that. When I think of the wine of Verona that we used to drink . . . !"

"Sometimes I dream of beer," Haupt said.

"München beer. Great barrels of it. Enough to swim in!"

"Two thousand or a whole army," Olive said, "what's the difference? Dead's dead. Here or Camerone." Moodily, he downed the clear raw liquid that the Mexicans distilled for a cactus brew and tried to make himself think it was good English gin. Drinking, to a legionnaire, was a serious business. It was not recreation or pleasure, it was as essential to life as eating and breathing.

Olive had been drinking steadily for almost two hours, ever since he had completed his tour of guard duty at the road barrier. He had started drinking in order to forget the brief affair with Sergent-Chef Ciano, but he hadn't forgotten. Ciano would let him think about it, and think about it, and finally when the incident actually had slipped out of Olive's mind . . .

Haupt struck the bar a shattering blow with his fist. "Beer!" he bellowed.

The proprietor came sidling out of the shadows like a startled spider. He was a frail, watery-eyed, nervous little man with a huge nose that quivered in futile indignation. Once, at least, there had been laughter in his cantina. Even when the bandits raided, his miserable hut had been alive with laughter. And the federal soldiers, and the firebrains of Juárez, and the plain citizens of Monterrey who were his friends, all of them had laughed while drinking. But not these legion-naires. They drank alone in sullen silence, or together they talked morosely, and occasionally one would explode in a fit of rage. But never was there any laughter.

The proprietor filled the German's glass with beer, the Italian's with the thin red wine of Neuvo León, the Englishman's with tequila. This army that they called *La Légion* was like no army the proprietor had ever seen before. Russians, Poles, Swedes, Spaniards. Men of every race and nationality. Why? What debt did these wretches owe to France that they must make payment in blood? What was an Italian doing in Mexico? Why was an Englishman fighting Juárez?

The proprietor sidled away from the bar and returned to the shadows.

"This wine is fit only for pickling herring!" Bello said angrily.

"A year from now," Olive told him, "it won't matter. We'll all be dead."

"I've heard that Bazaine's keeping a corridor open between Mexico City and Veracruz," Haupt said. "An escape route to the sea, if worst comes to worst."

Bello snorted. "A lot of good that will do us here in the north."

"Bazaine's an old legionnaire. He'll look after his own."

Olive and Bello turned pitying looks on the

credulous German. "A year from now we'll all be heroes," Olive said. "Like the heroes of Camerone."

As if by magic all their thoughts turned north. Mingled with anger and degradation and violence, some part of every legionnaire burned with the thought of desertion. Many attempted it in times of despair, or *cafard*, a form of madness peculiar to the Legion. Almost none succeeded. In Algeria there was a standing bounty for deserters. The Arabs collected one hundred francs for every deserter returned alive. One thousand francs for every deserter returned dead.

Bel-Abbès oddsmakers placed the chances of successful desertion at about a thousand to one. Here in Mexico, totally surrounded by hostiles, the odds seemed even poorer. And yet, more than one legionnaire had gazed hungrily to the north, toward the United States border . . .

"Forget it!" Olive said harshly to his comrades. "You wouldn't know what to do out of the Legion. Franz, could you return to München? And you, Leonardo, how would you be received in Italy? Providing you could get there. No better than I would be in Liverpool, if I'm any judge." Suddenly he laughed, but it was not a sound that the proprietor of the cantina recognized. "*A moi la Légion*!"

Bello and Haupt darted uneasy glances at the doorway. It was at times like this, between fights, that *cafard* struck most often. Olive saw the look that passed between them, and he did not blame them for their nervousness. Perhaps he was touched with the madness. For the past several hours he had examined the possibility of desertion from every side and had at last rejected it as impossible. Still, the thought nagged him.

Bello and Haupt quietly left Olive at the bar by himself. They were old soldiers and recognized the signs. If Olive meant to attempt something as insane as desertion, the less they saw of him the better.

Legionnaire Olive and the small dark spider of a barkeep were now alone in the cantina. The moment of madness would pass, Olive knew. It came and it went. All legionnaires experienced it.

Suddenly the shabby, dirt-floored room went dark. A huge figure stood in the doorway, blocking out the light. Olive was instantly aware of the menace in that room, the way an experienced soldier could tell the instant he moved into the enemy's field of fire. At first there was a knot of panic in his gut. But the panic was controlled, and soon it gave way to a kind of bleak fatalism.

"*Bon jour*, Legionnaire Olive." The iron figure of Sergent-Chef Giuseppe Ciano sauntered into the hut.

Olive wheeled and snapped to rigid attention. "*Bon jour*, Sergent-Chef Ciano!"

Ciano smiled. His nailhead teeth glistened.

17

Beneath his left arm he carried a crooked cane. He was clean-shaven, brushed, polished, gleaming, everything a soldier of France ought to be. He approached Olive, studying him as if he were some faintly amusing animal in a cage. He looked him up and down. He walked from side to side in the small room, inspecting Olive from every angle. He nodded from time to time and made little noises of satisfaction in his throat. And he smiled. Olive had the feeling that a four-inch shell could explode in the face of Sergent-Chef Ciano and that smile would never be disturbed.

"Enjoying a *pinard*, Legionnaire Olive?" Ciano asked pleasantly, glancing at Olive's empty glass.

"It's not *pinard*, sir. It's something they distill from cactus."

"From cactus!" The *sergent-chef* was fascinated. "Think of that. Life in the Legion is educational as well as pleasant, isn't it, Legionnaire Olive?"

"Yes, sir!" Olive said, maintaining his rigid attitude of attention.

"From cactus!" Ciano said again, amazed. Suddenly he clapped his hands. It was like a pistol shot in that small cantina. "You!" he shouted to the spider in the shadows, "I must have a glass of this nectar! What is it called, legionnaire?"

"Tequila, sir!"

"Two glasses of tequila!"

18

The little bar-keep scurried and wheezed and poured the drinks. The *sergent-chef* took the small glass in thick, calloused fingers and drank the fiery liquid without the smallest change of expression. "Slop," he pronounced. "Only pigs drink slop. Don't you know that, legionnaire?"

"Yes, sir!"

"Then drink it, Legionnaire Pig."

"Yes, sir!"

Olive reached for the second glass. His hand was shaking. He downed the tequila but spilled some over his chin.

"You drink your slop very well, legionnaire," Ciano said dryly. "Exactly like a pig." In what seemed to be the most casual of gestures he slapped Olive across the face.

To Olive it felt as if he had been clubbed with a musket butt. He felt his cheek burst on the inside and his mouth fill with blood. His head rang. For a moment his vision tilted crazily. The small glass had shattered in his hand and cut his chin. Blood, much darker and redder than Mexican wine, spattered his uniform. There was a knot in his throat. Salty tears of rage blurred his vision. But he did not move. He dropped his right hand quickly so that the thumb was alongside the trouser seam, and he maintained his muscle-straining position of attention.

"Look at your uniform, Legionnaire Olive," Ciano said sadly. "It is a disgrace to the Legion.

You are a disgrace to the Legion. Don't you agree?"

"Yes, sir!" Olive said hoarsely. This, he told himself, was nothing. He had seen men quietly, casually beaten into unconsciousness in a hundred little scenes just like this one. One had only to stand like stone, be blind and mute, do or say nothing—absolutely nothing—that could possibly offend the *sergent-chef*, and after a while it would be over.

Sergent-Chef Ciano smiled sadly. "Legionnaire," he said in a tone of despair, "I don't know what ought to be done about you. Truly, I don't know." He looked at Olive thoughtfully. He touched his square blue chin, pondering this unfair problem that had come to plague him. He paced to one side of the hut. He paced to the other. Then, in his preoccupation, he dropped his cane.

The cane clattered to the packed earth floor. "Sir!" Olive said automatically, and bent to retrieve the cane. Sergent-Chef Ciano struck him savagely between the shoulder blades and sent him sprawling.

Olive writhed on the floor, the breath knocked out of him. "Legionnaire," Ciano asked coldly, "did I give you permission to stand easy?"

"No, sir!" Olive managed to croak.

"Then get to your feet. Hand me my cane."

Olive fumbled for the cane and dragged himself

to his feet. Anger was a knot in his gut and a live coal in his throat. He stood at attention. Ciano shook his head from side to side in great distress. Olive's left cheek was already swollen, the eye was puffing and beginning to squint. He was covered with blood and filth. "Legionnaire," the *sergent-chef* said dejectedly, "look at yourself and tell me the truth. Be honest with me. Is that any way for a soldier of France to appear in a public place?"

"No, sir!" Olive said in an eerily constricted voice.

"You are a disgrace to the flag, not to mention the Legion and your company."

"Yes, sir!"

"What am I to do with you, Legionnaire Olive?"

"I don't know, sir!"

Sergent-Chef Ciano sighed. "I don't know, either." He began flicking the buttons of Olive's filthy uniform with the tip of his cane. "The problem would be simple," he said dreamily, "if you were fool enough to desert. I would simply kill you and that would be the end of it. You are a pig, and a particularly loathsome pig at that, but you are not such a fool as to attempt desertion. Are you, legionnaire?"

"No, sir!" Olive said hoarsely. The exploring tip of the cane moved from button to button. Suddenly the blunt wooden tip drove like a bullet into Olive's solar plexus. Olive gagged and bent double.

Sergent-Chef Ciano said sternly, "You are at attention, legionnaire."

Olive was momentarily paralyzed; he could not make himself stand erect.

With a sigh of resignation, the *sergent-chef* shifted hands with the cane and struck viciously across Olive's kidney.

The pain was blinding. Olive almost went to his knees but realized that such a thing would be a grave mistake. At the moment Ciano was merely working off some minor personal frustration, but if Olive were to collapse and the *sergent-chef* became angered . . . This was an eventuality that Legionnaire Olive would rather not dwell on. With a thin bright sword of pain running through his middle, Olive forced himself erect.

In the dirt street outside the cantina some legionnaires were singing again of their Empress in lyrics that would have singed Eugénie's delicate ears. A *sous-officier* put his head in the doorway and shouted, "Ciano, Echevesky's located a bathhouse! Hot water and real soap, even a woman to scrub your back for you!"

The *sergent-chef* considered, torn between two pleasures. After a moment he said, "I'll come with you." But before leaving he smiled at Olive. "We'll continue our little discussion some other time, legionnaire."

Ciano waited expectantly. Olive said quickly, "Yes, sir!" And the *sergent-chef* left the cantina a much happier and more relaxed person than he had been on entering it.

Olive fell against the bar, panting. Every muscle felt spongy and soft. He had an almost irresistible urge to start yelling, but he knew that if he ever started he wouldn't stop. That was *cafard*.

The scrawny little bar-keep, who had watched the strange scene with intense interest, sidled along the back side of the bar and quietly studied the legionnaire's grayish face.

"Tequila," Olive gasped.

The bar-keep shrugged, as if to say, "As long as you have money . . ." and filled another glass.

TWO

For the profession of man hunting Roger Trent had some outstanding qualifications. He had great patience, and he was perfectly willing to follow a trail wherever it led him, even to foreign countries. Also, he had experience on his side, and a dogged tenacity that sometimes passed as courage. And he was greedy. Of his several natural credentials, greed was by far the most important.

Trent liked to think of himself as thoroughly professional, and he was. He never became personally or emotionally involved. He had used the war years profitably as an agent with the Union Detective Agency in Chicago, where he had protected copperheads or tracked down enlistment bounty jumpers, as the particular assignment required.

Long before the end of the war Trent had started thinking about his future, and he correctly decided that the greatest opportunities would be found among the defeated, not the victors. Among the vanquished is where hate would be the strongest. Hate, as Roger Trent knew very well, was the lifeblood of a flourishing detective agency.

He was not an agency yet, but he had no doubt that one day Trent detectives would be as many and as powerful in the South as the Pinkertons were in the North. This was one other thing that Roger Trent had in abundance—self-confidence.

As an example of that confidence, he had already mentally added another thousand dollars to his growing savings account in Chicago. Experienced detectives developed an extraordinary set of senses which told them when the trail was narrowing, when a search was about to be concluded. Somehow he knew—without being able to say just how he knew—that the trail of Ward Cameron was ending here in Monterrey.

This feeling was so strong that Trent had carefully thought over the problem of whether to kill Cameron on the spot where he found him or try to get him back to Louisiana alive. Dead or alive, the bounty would be the same.

It would be infinitely simpler and safer to kill the man on sight. And probably more humane as well, although this had never been a consideration. On the other hand, it was sometimes difficult to prove death without a body—and it was a long, hot distance between Monterrey and Louisiana.

To tell the truth, there wouldn't be a great deal of profit in Cameron's return, no matter how it was accomplished. One thousand dollars, Union gold, was a lot of money, but this job was taking much longer than Trent had anticipated. He was anxious to get it over with. Two weeks ago when he first began to suspect that Cameron had slipped into Mexico mingled with a horde of ragtag Confederates, the wise thing would have been to confess failure and chalk Cameron down as a loss.

But Trent had his pride. And there was the long-range view to consider. He must think of this assignment as an investment, for he was at this very moment building the reputation of the future—Trent Detective Agency.

All the same, he would be much relieved to have the business over and done with. He did not like this country of Mexico, for one thing. The huddles of mud huts that passed as villages were eerily silent. Along the roads there were only women and children to be seen—everyone else had flocked to Juárez. Over Monterrey an invisible cloud of hostility seemed to hover.

For Trent the camp of sullen Confederates near the southern edge of Monterrey was even more depressing than the town. He had not dared question those men, any one of whom could have been an old army comrade of Cameron's. However, Trent had a plan.

It was near midafternoon when the detective reined his sturdy roan gelding through the litter of Monterrey's almost deserted streets. He headed for the oldest and most decrepit part of the town, where the stench was strongest, the flies thickest, where all the women were hags and the liquor was raw and cheap. Here, as he had anticipated, he found the off-duty legionnaires.

The future president of the Trent Detective Agency sat his saddle a little straighter and smiled.

He dismounted in front of a long line of miserable adobe huts, leaving the roan at a rack in ankle-deep dust. He thoughtfully removed his almost-new, fifteen-shot Henry from the saddle boot. If necessary, he would risk having his horse and rig stolen, but not his rifle. He made for the first hut.

"Anybody here speak English?"

The bar-keep and a hag stared at him blankly. Two Russian legionnaires, intent on their drinking, were not curious enough to look up.

It was in the fourth cantina that a rugged, blunt-featured legionnaire regarded him suspiciously and said in the clipped, harsh accent of the Liverpool dock worker, "What do you want?"

Trent smiled to himself. Somehow he knew that he had found his man. "I need to talk to some of these Mexicans about a . . . personal matter. But I don't speak the language. Do you understand Spanish?"

Legionnaire Second Class William Olive caressed his bruised face and spat a trace of blood on the dirt floor. "In the Legion you learn a little of everything. What do you want to talk about?"

Trent ignored the probe. "I'll tell you later, if and when we strike a deal. Are you free? I mean, are you off duty for the rest of the day?"

Olive nodded. He remembered where he had seen this man before, this well-fed man on a well-fed horse, carrying an expensive repeating rifle in his saddle scabbard. Now the rifle rested in the crook of Trent's arm.

"I need an interpreter," Trent told him. "I expect you'll do well enough."

"Interpreter!" The notion seemed to amuse Legionnaire Olive. "What's it worth to you?"

Trent rubbed his chin thoughtfully. "One dollar American now. Another when you've finished. It shouldn't take more than an hour or so."

Two American dollars! That was more than a legionnaire earned in an entire month! He yelled to the bar-keep, and the spidery little man scuttled out of the shadows and filled two glasses with tequila.

For the sake of appearances Trent touched the liquid fire to his lips and set the glass down. Olive drank his at one gulp. "All right," he said, now that the formalities had been observed. "Legionnaire Olive knows this stinkin' town inside-out and backwards. What is it you want, a woman?"

Trent did not try to conceal his disgust. "A

man," he said coldly. "A particular man." From the pocket of his officer's coat he took out a small bundle of papers. Olive knew immediately what this man was and what he wanted.

He pushed the papers away and said sharply, "Put them away!"

Trent looked at him blankly. The legionnaire said quietly, motioning for another tequila, "In the Legion a lot of men get killed. It's mean, dirty work and the pay's the lowest in the world. Where do you figure the Legion gets the recruits to keep its ranks filled?" Olive smiled faintly. "They grab them a step ahead of the Paris *flics*, or the English constables, or maybe Scotland Yard. You walk the streets of Monterrey, see all the white kepis goin' up and down? Nine out of ten of them wanted by the police someplace. Bounty hunters, as you call them, do not last long around a group of legionnaires."

Trent was not interested in the problems of these white-capped misfits. "The man I'm looking for is a United States citizen, not a legionnaire."

Olive studied his man with slitted eyes. He groped for a figure which, to a legionnaire, would mean almost unbelievable wealth. "All right," he said. "But the risks are higher than I counted on. And so's the charge. Ten dollars it'll be now. All in advance."

Trent's eyes glittered. He said flatly, "I don't

like being threatened. And I believe that's what you're trying to do."

Legionnaire William Olive, who on lonely outposts had faced terrors that this American could not even imagine, was not intimidated. "Ten dollars," he said again. "Or would you rather I passed the word that an American bounty hunter . . ."

Trent turned faintly purple. Olive smiled, waited, and finally took the small, thin gold piece that the detective proffered.

They moved to a table, where Olive had a look at the posters. Trent did not bother to show his credentials; the packet of federal arrest warrants, the temporary assignment to the office of deputy U.S. marshal.

Olive went through the posters slowly. Suddenly he whistled and looked sharply at Trent. "One thousand dollars! What crime could a man have done that would make him so valuable!"

"The crime of murder," Trent said coldly, "and other offenses against the military government of Louisiana."

Olive grinned widely. "I remember a Berber settlement that the Legion 'pacified' once. A stinkin' little place—Arac-Ar, they called it. Our company left a squad there to keep order. The head man, the old sheik, was a troublemaker, so we killed him. Then we had to kill his brothers and some of his pals. Finally we found a new head man that would march in line and do like we told him. But we found him one morning with his throat cut, turned around so that he was facing Rome. Worst thing that can happen to a believer." Olive sighed. "We found another head man, but he didn't last. Then we killed some more Arabs, and two legionnaires got their throats cut. Finally we got word from Bel-Abbès that the pacification of the Berbers had been a great success and we were released and sent back to the company."

The point of Olive's story was clear enough, but Trent was not interested. "Have you seen any of those men here in Monterrey?" He indicated the posters.

Olive looked again. On four of the posters there were detailed descriptions of the wanted men. But mere specifications, no matter how detailed, could not tell what a man was like. The remaining two had pictures of the criminals. Someone had gone to a great deal of trouble over those pictures. The artists' drawings had been taken from old daguerreotypes. The engraving and printing were highly competent, and even the paper was of passable quality.

The first man, whose name was Sunderson, was also a murderer, according to the text. He was young and sharp-eyed and looked ill-tempered and impulsive. The Legion was full of such Sundersons, but Olive had never seen this particular one before.

The thousand-dollar murderer was an altogether different proposition. Wardson Lee Cameron. Six feet, one inch tall. Weight one hundred and seventy pounds. Age . . . he looked in his middle thirties, but war could do things to a man's looks. He wore a Confederate officer's uniform. There was an unmistakable toughness about him that neither camera nor artist's pen did anything to soften. He looked as if he had been soaked in brine and cured in the sun. He might have been an old-time *sous-officier* in the Legion. Or possibly a regimental commander who had been promoted from the ranks.

Olive said at last, "This must be your man."

"Cameron's the important one. Have you ever seen him?"

". . . No."

"You're not sure?"

"There's something about him." Olive shrugged. "No, I've never seen him."

"If I have judged correctly," Trent said, "he would have made Monterrey perhaps five, six days ago."

"Maybe he's with the camp of Americans south of town."

Trent shook his head. "No, it's too obvious. And anyway, I've been there."

"What do you want me to do? Show the picture to Mexicans, see if anybody knows him?"

"No. As you pointed out," Trent said dryly,

"bounty hunters are not so very popular here. However, there are some details not shown in the picture or mentioned in the text. For instance, there is a long scar along Cameron's left cheek, an old dueling souvenir. His nose, as you can see, is rather long and hooked; at one time it was broken and improperly set."

The detective closed his eyes for a moment, picturing his prey in his mind. "Cameron comes," he said, "from what is known—or used to be known—as southern aristocracy. He's an expert shot with pistol and rifle and, I am told, a fine horseman. At one time his family raised jumpers and Thoroughbreds."

Olive scowled and gazed around at the miserable little cantina. "You expect to find an aristocrat in a place like this?"

Trent smiled, and clearly it was not something that he did often. "Southern aristocracy is as dead as the patricians of Rome."

Legionnaire Olive sat for a moment, puzzled.

Trent made a quick decision. He placed two gold double eagles on the edge of the table. "Forty dollars of purest gold," he told the legionnaire. "They're yours the instant you find Cameron and take me to him."

Olive stared at the small gold disks. He could not fairly comprehend the extent of such massive wealth except in terms of wine—barrels of wine, oceans of it, the blood-red *pinard* of Sidi-bel-

Abbès. He glanced at Trent, then at the coins. He licked his dry lips. "You don't want an interpreter, then."

"No. My asking questions, even of Mexicans, would be taking an unnecessary risk. Do we have a bargain?"

"What if Cameron isn't in Monterrey?"

"He's here."

"What if I can't find him?"

Trent picked up the coins and fanned them between his thumb and forefinger, as if they were the winning pair of aces.

"You'll find him. When you do I'll be waiting for you here."

Wardson Lee Cameron lay on his back soberly studying the activity of a large gray spider in the corner of his room. The spider was working busily to spin the web in which he would catch flies. Then he could take it easy. Lead the life of leisure, like a country squire. Sit back and rock and sip minted bourbon while everything he needed popped right into his net.

Mexico, Cameron decided, must be a fine place for spiders. Certainly there were more than enough flies to go around.

He wasn't so sure about ex-country squires and soldiers of the Confederacy.

The room was a small hollow cube with a knife blade of light slanting through a narrow window;

it contained a grass-filled mattress, a gray spider, a regiment of flies, and Cameron. This is where he had been for three days, ever since Corporal Richards had rejoined his old outfit, bringing word that Trent had picked up Cameron's scent in Laredo and was no doubt making for Monterrey.

Hiding out in a church had not been Cameron's idea; he had wanted very much to meet this detective. The church had been Colonel Montfort's idea.

It had been the colonel's fear that a showdown between Cameron and a representative of the military government in Ayersville would jeopardize his plans for the entire regiment. The French wanted the Confederate soldiers badly enough, but they were fearful that the United States would enter the war on the side of Juárez. The last thing they wanted was to antagonize the great power to the North. There was even talk of pulling the Foreign Legion out of Monterrey, at least until Maximilian was a bit more secure in his role as Emperor of Mexico.

Which, in Cameron's judgment, might be never. His confidence in French arms was waning. A kind of gray ash had settled on that rosy dream of creating a powerful new Confederate army here in Mexico. When a captain of Confederate cavalry had to hide from a private detective—and in a foreign country at that . . .

There was a nervous little rapping on the door

of his cell. That would be Maria. He wasn't quite sure who Maria was, except that she was a brassy little wench who brought his meals and had a great many other things to offer. But Cameron wasn't interested. It was at that moment that Cameron realized that, over a period of weeks, he had been slowly, quietly losing interest in almost everything.

Maria broke into the room, grinning widely. Colonel Montfort towered behind the girl. Then he entered the room, swept the girl out the door, and threw the latch. In the presence of his commanding officer, Cameron lurched to his feet.

"In God's house," Montfort said, "I hope you haven't forgotten to behave yourself."

In this bare square of a cell Cameron had almost forgotten that he was in a church. The colonel had spoken to a French officer in Monterrey who, in turn, had spoken to the priest, and that was how Cameron had come to be here. "Yes, sir," he said, grinning weakly, "I've behaved myself."

Colonel Montfort was not merely Cameron's commanding officer; in the years before the war the Montfort plantation had joined the Cameron land, two show places of Ayers County. They had shared an experience, the war; and a vision, the Confederacy.

At the moment Cameron wanted to hear one thing—that the regiment was ready to join Bazaine in the south. But the colonel shook his head. "Not just yet. The French are nervous; the government in Washington is reckless and drunk with power now that it has the Confederacy under its heel. The French can't afford . . ."

It was an old story and Cameron had already heard it too many times. He experienced that same yawning sickness that he had known at Gettysburg when he had finally realized that the war was lost. There was Montfort, his left sleeve hanging empty, a remembrance of The Wilderness. The colonel had spent the last days of the war in pain and delirium, and he still didn't realize how thoroughly the South had been crushed. His faith in the rebirth of the Confederacy was infectious. Cameron himself had been stricken by it—but now the fever was slowly leaving him.

"A little time, Ward," Montfort was saying with fatherly sternness. "Have a little faith and patience."

"Yes, sir," Cameron said dutifully.

The colonel passed his hand over his bearded chin. He was thin, and his face was a neutral gray, like the adobe huts of Mexico. Once he had been a big, bluff man overflowing with life. "We think," he said at last, "that the detective is in Monterrey."

Cameron was instantly alert. "There's a man I would like to meet."

Colonel Montfort shook his head angrily. "That must not happen! We, the men of the regiment, will attend to Mr. Trent. Very quietly, with no fuss. By the time the new officials at Ayersville realize what has happened we will be in Puebla with Bazaine."

"If Trent can be found. We've known about him almost from the day the military government hired him. But here he is, in Monterrey."

"We think."

Cameron grinned.

"I oughtn't to have come here," the colonel said, "but I had to get your word, as an officer and a gentleman, that you would let me, and the regiment, handle this."

Once a simple order would have sufficed, but now the word of an officer and gentleman was needed. This seemed to shed a certain bleakness on the affair, but Cameron decided that he would rather not explore it. He said, "You have my word, sir."

Colonel Montfort beamed with affection. "I knew I could count on you. This mess will be cleaned up soon, you have *my* word on that. We'll be the old regiment again, a fighting regiment. The beginning of better things, Ward. Much better things!"

"Yes, sir," Cameron said again. If there was a certain dryness to his tone, the colonel apparently did not hear it.

Legionnaire William Olive was overwhelmed at the power in one small piece of gold. Gold, translated into liquor, was doubly powerful. But neither gold nor liquor could help a man if he had not the brains to use them efficiently. Legionnaire Olive was not one to make frontal attacks on unassailable fortresses. Sit a minute, think it over. When this philosophy sifted down to the level of the French general staff there would be fewer Legion graves and more live legionnaires. In the meantime he would apply his reasoning to the problem at hand.

First, Olive attempted to put himself in the fugitive's place. A fugitive in Monterrey. Where would he go? To his old outfit at the Confederate camp? No. He agreed with the bounty hunter that this was too dangerous. Cameron would have to stay under wraps as long as he was this close to the border. Or until the detective was eliminated.

This was what Olive feared most. The elimination of Trent would see the two golden double eagles flying right out of the legionnaire's eager grasp.

But where could an ex-Confederate hide in a hostile country? It would be very difficult unless . . . Of course. Cameron must have had assistance from the French command in Monterrey. This was altogether possible, even probable. Olive could see the scene now. A

Confederate commander saying politely but firmly to the French recruiter: "Sir, if you desire the cooperation of my unit, I must insist . . ."

That would do it. The French recruiting officer would think of something.

Olive was well satisfied with his examination of the problem up to this point. Now he needed help. And this is where he discovered the power of gold.

Legionnaire Olive began a systematic search of the mud hut cantinas, and at last he found the *cabot-chef* of the recruiting detachment in Monterrey. Corporals, even chief corporals, were not of that exalted group, the *sous-officiers*. Nevertheless, a corporal, in the eyes of a common legionnaire, stood only slightly below the pinnacle of the true gods, the sergeants.

Olive approached his objective as cautiously as a new Saint-Cyr graduate advancing on a Berber strongpoint. Corporal Karel Durchiez, the cantina's lone customer, occupied one of the five tables in the place. There was no bar. He was staring moodily, with unfocused anger, at the glass of wine which sat before him. Olive entered the place, his kepi set jauntily on the back of his head. "*Pinard*," he said loudly to the hostile Mexican who owned the place. "Good red wine," he added in Legion Spanish. "Not the slop you serve legionnaires and call wine."

The owner glared. With a flourish Olive

dumped a clanging pile of silver on a table not far from Corporal Durchiez. Both Durchiez and the cantina proprietor were startled at this display of wealth. Olive looked at the Mexican and started to scoop up the money. What an amazing lot of silver a small piece of gold could buy! "All right, if you'd rather drink your good wine yourself, maybe the next cantina will be more obliging."

The proprietor made a little sound of panic. "No, no! Sit, take a table! I will serve you!"

"Real wine, now!"

"You will not be disappointed!" He tore his gaze away from the mound of silver and scurried to what appeared to be a heap of rubble in the back of the hut. He returned with a dirty glass and a bottle which he opened grudgingly. Olive took up the cork, inspected it, sniffed it critically, as he had seen French officers do whenever a bottle from one of the great vineyards of France was opened.

Olive slopped some of the wine into the glass. The proprietor winced as though it had been his blood. The legionnaire gulped the wine and smacked his lips. "Very sound," he said, with a knowing nod. "Excellent body. Plenty of alcohol, but not too much. Good color." He held it to the light and studied it through the filthy glass.

While pulling mess duty in Sidi-bel-Abbès, he had seen the officers do it this way. "Of course it doesn't have the finesse of a Lafite, or the fleshiness of a good Pomerol, or breed of, say, of a fine Margaux . . ." The owner was looking at him in a peculiar way, and Olive was afraid that he had overdone it. Suddenly he laughed. "Anyhow, it's an honest drink, and as good as the wine of Algeria." Which was true.

He appeared to see Durchiez for the first time. "It seems a shame," he said, "to drink good wine by oneself. Corporal-Chef, would you care to join me?"

Corporal Durchiez wiped a hand across his mouth and eyed the wine thirstily. It was not his habit to fraternize with second-class legionnaires. "All right," he condescended, "I guess I don't mind." He dashed his own insipid vintage to the floor and moved to Olive's table.

Olive filled his grass brim full. "*La Légion*!"

"*La Légion*!" They emptied their glasses.

A kind of solemn bliss came over the corporal's face as the full-bodied wine flowed down his throat and soothed his stomach. "Of course," he said, "it's nowhere near good Algerian."

"But it's better than nothing."

To this the corporal was forced to agree. They saluted again.

"Bel-Abbès!"

"The wine and the women of Algiers!"

"May all these Mexicans rot in hell. And Maximilian with them!"

"Bring another bottle of the same!" Olive said to the cantina owner. "Make it two bottles!"

Toward the end of the second bottle they were old comrades. Corporal's rank was forgotten. Nevertheless, Durchiez kept eyeing the scattered silver with extraordinary interest.

Olive grinned and went through the motions of dealing cards. "Once in a lifetime luck and cards run with a man."

"A lifetime in the Legion," Durchiez observed, "can be very short. Did you have comrades at Camerone?"

Olive nodded. They drank. They toasted *La Légion*, which they both cursed every day of their lives. But it was all they had. *A moi la Légion*. Olive ordered another bottle.

At the beginning of the fourth bottle Olive guided the conversation to Durchiez's recruiting assignment. The corporal shook his head sadly. "Perhaps our friends the Confederates fought well enough in their own war, but they are miserably unprofessional."

"Bazaine must think well of them."

"Bazaine is not the old legionnaire he once was. If a man is capable of holding a rifle or musket, Marshal Bazaine thinks well of him. I think Marshal Bazaine is interested only in armed rabble, not soldiers. Someone to keep the corridor to Veracruz open. One fine day our Marshal Bazaine will board a waiting ship and sail for France, leaving old Maximilian to face the firing squad by himself."

A corporal, or any legionnaire, would need to be very drunk to voice such thoughts. Olive, who had slowed his drinking considerably after the second bottle, said gently, "I don't suppose your commanders associate much with these Confederates—socially, I mean."

Durchiez snorted. "What's the sense of associating with cannon fodder. In a month they'll all be dead. You know, I think they all hate our guts. But they've got this crazy notion about rebuilding their army. *Cafard*!"

"Still," Olive said, "many of them are of good families. Old families, with their origins in France."

The corporal had sunk into a bleary fuzziness in which everything was pleasantly unreal. "Yes," he said after a long silence. "There was an old colonel, lost an arm in some battle called The Wilderness. My captain—Captain Decherf—received him with more courtesy than . . ."

The corporal was beginning to leave sentences unfinished. His thoughts were slowly sinking in a pleasant ooze.

Olive prodded him. "What about the old colonel?"

Durchiez grinned crookedly. "Threatened to pull his whole regiment out of Mexico if he didn't . . ."

"Didn't what?"

"One of his officers. Man with a name like yours, English. Or Scotch, maybe."

Olive began to smile. "Cameron?"

"That's it. Almost the same as the battle. Camerone—Cameron."

"What about Cameron?"

"Nothing. Hell, I don't know. You don't think captains and colonels tell *me* what they're thinking, do you? Is there any more of that wine?"

It had been a very expensive afternoon, but worth every centime. Olive paid for another bottle and reeled out of the cantina.

THREE

Legionnaire Second Class William Olive staggered along the street of bordellos and cantinas. Hags grabbed at him as he made his uncertain way toward the adobe hut where his squad was billeted. But Legionnaire Olive was not in the mood for women. And he had already had too much wine. From time to time he would pause and rest against an adobe wall and try to clear the mist from his brain.

Finding the old one-armed colonel ought to be a simple matter. Olive felt certain that Colonel Montfort, sooner or later, would lead him to Cameron. Cameron and the two golden double eagles.

But now he turned his gaze up to the sullen sky. In about one hour he would be walking his guard post, brushed and polished and shaved and every inch a legionnaire. Off duty he was free to do about as he pleased, but when the Legion beckoned, the other world ceased to exist.

Drunk or sober, sick or well, the legionnaire did his duty. And today it was Olive's duty to stand his guard and protect the citizens of Monterrey and the men of the Third Battalion and, above all else, do it in such a way as to gladden the heart of Sergent-Chef Giuseppe Ciano.

Therefore, Olive forced himself to forget the bounty hunter's twin disks of gold, and he put the old colonel and the man called Cameron out of his mind. *La Légion* required his services.

As William Olive walked his guard post with pounding head and churning stomach, Roger Trent quietly waited. He sat at his table in the shabby little cantina, from time to time sipping a little of the unpleasant wine.

At last, when Trent was satisfied that he would not be seeing William Olive that night, he left the cantina. More than one legionnaire had fallen to the dirt or sat sprawled against an adobe wall, dead drunk and snoring. Had it been men like these who had fought so valiantly at Camerone against overwhelming odds? Incredible!

The detective slipped his Henry into the saddle boot, mounted his roan and reined south.

The veterans of the Confederate camp outside Monterrey thought of Trent, if they thought of him at all, as a loner. Most of the men looked for others to share their misery with. Remnants of army outfits tended to mess together, hashing over old battles and cursing the carpetbaggers, the turncoats, and the tax collectors.

But there were the loners too—men so filled with hate that they couldn't bear to talk about the war or its aftermath. These were men who had come from war to find their homes in ashes, their crops ruined, their animals slaughtered or taken for taxes, their families scattered and often dead. These were the men who messed by themselves, subsisting on parched corn and the few things they could steal—and their hate.

The detective staked his roan near the edge of the encampment. He did not understand these men any more than he had understood the drunken legionnaires. They meant nothing to him, their miseries were of no concern to him.

He looked forward to the next day. He had great confidence in Olive's ability to eventually locate Cameron for him. With no problems that could not be solved and no doubts to disturb him, Trent sank into deep and restful sleep.

From the tiny cubicle situated directly below the bell tower of the Cathedral Saint Mark, Father Ignatius detected a highly unecclesiastical feminine giggle. The sound both shocked and angered him. There was nothing he could do about it directly. He registered his outrage by marching back and forth in front of the door, his heavy-soled sandals clopping like unshod hooves on the stone floor.

Father Ignatius was not political. He had not wanted to give the American, who was obviously a wanted criminal in his own land, sanctuary in

Saint Mark. Anyway, there was no such thing as a sanctuary any more.

But the French officer had made it quite clear. "Father, if it should become necessary for French forces to evacuate Monterrey, naturally certain precautions would have to be seen to. For instance, the bell tower of this beautiful cathedral. The enemy would surely use it as a post from which to observe our movements. Routine military considerations dictate that such strongpoints be eliminated—I'm afraid the best part of your church would have to be blown up."

Father Ignatius' face had gone white. "You could not! You would not dare!"

"Military necessity, Father," the Frenchman had replied. "However . . ."

Blandly, the officer had explained. Hide the American and protect him, and the ancient church would not be reduced to rubble. With great distaste, Father Ignatius had admitted the American, Cameron. But he had not bargained for this brazen wench, Maria, who brought the fugitive his meals and perhaps gave other services besides!

He need not have worried. Cameron was as edgy as a caged wolf. He paced back and forth before the narrow window, only half listening to Maria's chatter about her mother, the best cook in Mexico; her three sisters, the most beautiful

49

women in Mexico, next to Maria herself, of course; her four brothers, all of whom were fighting with Juárez and whose bravery was legend. Cameron's thoughts were hundreds of miles away, at a place known as Liveoak, a stately white house with a great covered gallery that often accommodated more than a hundred guests. And a thousand acres of lush green land in the rich heart of Louisiana.

He paused in front of the slit window and stared out at the gray-white huts and buildings of Monterrey, a place that he was rapidly learning to hate. Strange, he couldn't even remember what Stuart Jeffers looked like. He just barely remembered shooting him.

He became aware of Father Ignatius' heavy tread on the other side of the door. "Time you got out of here," he said to Maria. When she started to pout he gave her an offhand whack across the rear, which accounted for the giggle. He gathered up the dishes in which she had brought his supper and thrust them into the girl's arms. "Tell your mother easier on the pepper next time," he said, opening the door and propelling her almost into the arms of the good father.

Cameron did not try to explain, for it would have been impossible. Instead he said pleasantly, "Evenin', Father." But he said it to the broad back of the priest, who was beating an outraged retreat.

Cameron returned to his room. Inactivity, after four years of thunder and fury, rubbed his nerves raw. He wanted to be in camp with his fellow officers, waiting, as they had done so often before, for the next campaign. This time it was marching orders from Bazaine that they were waiting for, but the place and the enemy didn't seem so very important now.

Sergent-Chef Giuseppe Ciano was not in a happy mood. Even for a *sous-officier* of the Legion, his mood was unusually dark. His head pounded, his insides burned, and his pockets were empty. The company had not been paid for three months. His luck, usually very good, had suddenly gone sour, and he had lost his last centime gambling with fellow *sous-officiers*.

On top of that, in this land of hostile beauties and greedy hags, he had lost a very acceptable dark-eyed wench by the name of Carmela to a horse-faced lieutenant in the recruiting detachment. The lieutenant, of course, like many of the regular officers, came from a wealthy family and did not have to live on Legion pay.

Strangely, these misfortunes did not rankle him nearly as much as a story told to him by a *cabot-chef* of that same infamous recruiting detachment. According to this corporal, a certain Legionnaire William Olive had plied him with oceans of wine—full, red wine as good as the best Algerian. Ciano could not believe it. Where would a second-class legionnaire get money for anything but the cheapest kind of colored slop? And yet the corporal swore to the truth of the story, and certainly the man's magnificently bloodshot eyes and wilted manner had added authenticity to the tale.

The longer Sergent-Chef Ciano thought about it, the more he was inclined to believe that the corporal had been telling the truth. Ciano, his own head pounding from the cheapest of wines, went into a cold rage when he imagined Olive, a thousand times his inferior, sopping up decent drink. It would be very interesting, he decided, to discover just how Olive came by the money for such a bacchanal. Sergent-Chef Ciano would make it his duty and his pleasure to expose Olive's little mystery.

But Legionnaire Olive seemed to have disappeared after completing his guard tour at the road barrier. The men who billeted with him did not know where he had gone. Sergent-Chef Ciano told himself that these private affairs of a common legionnaire were of no importance and that it was beneath the dignity of a *sous-officier* to lavish it with so much attention.

The argument was sound, but Ciano was in no mood to listen. It infuriated him further when he failed to find Olive in one of his usual haunts. As the day wore on and the hot sun bore down on his pounding head the desire to find Olive became an obsession.

From fellow *sous-officiers* he borrowed money for wine, and he moodily drank the cheapest swill available. He considered his problem. Then, when the money was gone, the problem was still there but he was viciously drunk. He remembered the corporal whose name was Durchiez, but he could not find Durchiez either. He grew hotter and angrier and more determined. Finally, as the fiery Mexican sun was beginning to set, he found Olive.

His first impulse was to confront Olive immediately and demand to know where he had stolen the money for lavishing *cabot-chefs* with good wine, for he was certain now that Olive had stolen the money from his fellow legionnaires. In the Legion, theft was the one serious crime and was dealt with accordingly. Sometimes the thief was merely beaten to bloody unconsciousness. Sometimes he was crucified or spiked to the barracks floor with bayonets. Or, if the victims of the theft were feeling especially merciful, they might kill him outright.

But Ciano curbed his first impulse. He noted that Legionnaire Olive was behaving in a queer and suspicious manner. He would walk rapidly, staring fixedly straight ahead, and then he would pause and suddenly flatten himself against an adobe hut or in a doorway. Then he would move on again, almost at double time.

Well ahead of Olive one of the Confederates—an officer with an empty left sleeve—was riding a black Thoroughbred through the twisting Monterrey street. From time to time he would cast an uneasy glance over his shoulder. It was at these times, Sergent-Chef Ciano noticed, that Olive tried to make himself invisible.

Obviously Legionnaire Olive was following the one-armed Confederate, and he didn't want the Confederate to know that he was being followed. Ciano found this development intriguing.

As Olive followed the one-armed officer, Sergent-Chef Ciano followed Olive. He felt ridiculous doing it, but this was just one more grievance that he could add to the long list that he was mentally compiling against the legionnaire. The odd procession made its way through unfamiliar streets, out of the section of low cantinas and bordellos.

Surprisingly, the twisting passage ended directly in front of a large gray cathedral. The Confederate dismounted and left his horse opposite the cathedral. Foolish, Ciano thought to himself. A valuable animal like that. Maybe that was Olive's game, trailing the Confederate until he dismounted and then stealing the horse.

But that wasn't it. Olive had made himself invisible by leaning drunkenly against an adobe wall. Drunken legionnaires were as common as mud huts in Monterrey.

Again the one-armed officer looked back over his shoulder. Then he climbed the stone steps of the cathedral. Olive watched with apparent fascination as the Confederate slipped beneath the Gothic arch and disappeared in the deep shadow.

Olive moved into a dark doorway, still gazing fixedly at the cathedral. Curiosity had the better of Sergent-Chef Ciano. What was Olive up to if not to steal the officer's horse or equipment? He forced himself to watch quietly a while longer.

Perhaps four or five minutes passed and, in that darkened doorway, Legionnaire Olive had not made a move. Olive's fascination for that cathedral was infectious. The *sergent-chef* found himself staring at it, waiting for something, he couldn't guess what. Then, for a moment, a light flared in a slitted window directly beneath the bell tower and went out almost immediately.

It could have been a match, held just long enough to light a cigar, perhaps, and then put out. Or it could have been a signal.

Whatever it had been, Olive reacted to it. He stepped out of the doorway and hurried back up the twisting street. Dusk was just coming down on Monterrey. Sergent-Chef Giuseppe Ciano lounged in an alleyway about a hundred yards away. Olive was coming toward him at the brisk gait of an old-time legionnaire. The *sergent-chef* let him come.

Father Ignatius guided the one-armed American up the stone staircase that led to the bell tower. He wanted to complain about the servant girl, Maria, who brought food to the man called Cameron. But these Americans did not understand Spanish, and the priest knew little English. In the end he let the matter go unmentioned. At last they reached the door to Cameron's cell-like room, and Father Ignatius bowed with Latin politeness and vanished.

Colonel Montfort rapped on the door. "Ward?"

The door opened almost immediately. "I know," the colonel said before Cameron could speak, "I shouldn't have come. But I'm sure I wasn't followed. We've located the detective—one of them, anyway—and he's sitting in a cantina where he's been since we first discovered him. But that doesn't matter now. Your time of hiding is over."

Cameron could hardly believe it. "You're sure?"

"We strike tomorrow for Zacatecas."

"That's official?"

"Well, not official, but it's common knowledge. You must be the only one in Monterrey who doesn't know about it."

Cameron did not have much faith in rumors, common knowledge or not. But he was so tired of this bare room that he could make himself believe anything. "That's good news. I don't have anything against churches, but I've got to admit I'm getting a little sick of this one."

The colonel laughed softly and stepped into the room which was as dark as a bat cave. Cameron closed the door and threw the latch. Secrecy had come to be a habit with him. "Here," Montfort said, touching Cameron's shoulder. "A little something to celebrate your freedom with."

The colonel pressed a cigar into Cameron's hand. "The last of the box that I brought with me. Virginia tobacco; the last we'll see for a long while, I expect."

Cameron struck a match. When the flame was blown out they could see each other by the glowing tips of their cigars.

"The regiment's really pulling out. . . . The notion's a little hard to get used to."

"Of course," the colonel said, "the carpet-baggers will still be after your hide, but I doubt they'll probe deeper than Monterrey. If they do, we'll know how to deal with them. Everything's settled between the regiment and Marshal Bazaine."

"And the detective in the cantina?"

"I've agreed to let the French handle him. These Foreign Legionnaires are old hands at dealing with agents and traitors. He'll simply . . . disappear."

That made it a little hard on detectives, Cameron thought wryly. But when you took sides in a war the stakes were high. And as far as Montfort and many others were concerned, the Confederacy's war was far from over—indeed, it was just beginning.

"Well," Montfort said, "I just wanted to tell you myself. You won't mind staying here one more night, will you?"

"Whatever you think best, sir. When can I expect to pull out?"

"First light, most likely. Everybody's standing by, waiting for marching orders. All your gear is in the headquarters wagon." They stood for a moment, feeling that something was being left unsaid but not knowing what. "I'll send a man for you," the colonel said, "as soon as we're sure the way is clear. The French will . . . attend to the detective tonight."

"What if the detective isn't alone?"

Montfort hesitated. Cameron seemed to see him smile, but it was not a happy expression. "The legionnaires will question him. They assure me that this man, whose name is Trent, will tell them all about any assistants that might be with him. Legionnaires are very efficient at this sort of thing—the Berber warriors in Africa were their teachers." He gestured with his cigar, as if pushing the thought away. This was not his kind of war. "At any rate, we'll know that Trent will

58

leave no back trail to Louisiana. Or Washington."
Then, excessively brisk, "Goodnight, Ward. Until
tomorrow."

"Until tomorrow, Colonel."

When Montfort was gone Cameron stood
staring at the rosy tip of his cigar. Because of
the bounty on his head in the States, Cameron
had more reason than most men for throwing
in with the French and for holding to the cause
that so many good men had died for. But a
vague sense of unreality had enveloped him
the moment he crossed the Bravo and entered
Mexico. Here he was a stranger—he had trouble
remembering what the *cause* had been and what
it had meant. No matter how you spelled it, he
was a fugitive, a mercenary, a blood brother to
those legionnaires who sought sanctuary in the
profession of arms.

Now the feeling of unreality was almost complete. The war that he now found himself in was
no kind of war that he could recognize. A war of
stealth and torture and silent murder. Lord knew
there had been blood enough at The Wilderness,
Spotsylvania, Peachtree Creek, and Jonesboro,
but there had also been honor.

A strange word in this year of hate and anger,
this red summer of 1865. Honor.

From the slit of the window Cameron gazed
down at the town. It looked white and clean now,
washed in the light of a full moon. A foreign

town, a foreign country. And tomorrow he would be marching and perhaps fighting for a foreign flag.

Sergent-Chef Ciano lay flat against the adobe wall, out of sight. He listened to the thuds of Legionnaire Olive's heavy marching boots coming toward him. At exactly the right moment he stepped into the street, directly in the legionnaire's path.

The *sergent-chef* grinned widely. He spoke in French, because all *sous-officiers* prided themselves, no matter what their nationality, on their ability to speak flawless French. "Well now, Legionnaire Olive, you have been contemplating the cathedral. Perhaps you were tempted to confess your sins to a priest, eh? Very well, you may consider me your priest. Confess to me your sin—the sin of theft. I have always been kind, have I not? Kind, gentle, understanding? Much better you confess to me than to your comrades whom you have robbed."

Legionnaire Olive stood frozen, sick and dumb and empty-gutted with fear. Under normal conditions, which in the Legion meant war, William Olive was far from being a coward. If the Legion had been a unit to take note of such details, it might well have singled him out for acts of bravery. If it was not bravery, it amounted to the same thing, that fatalistic disregard for life which the Legion instilled in its fighting men. But the Legion also taught fear.

Sergent-Chef Ciano held his broad smile. Olive saw that Ciano was drunk, but this neither increased nor diminished his fear. "Well, Legionnaire Olive, what have you to say for yourself?"

Olive swallowed with difficulty. He wanted to lick his dry lips, but he knew that Ciano would take any such action as a major afront.

The *sergent-chef* waited with an elaborate show of patience. He didn't mind waiting, now that he had found his man at last. In fact, he rather enjoyed the way a legionnaire's face went from red to chalk white to ashy gray.

Some years in the future a Russian, experimenting with dogs, would discover a principle called "conditioned reflex," blissfully unaware that armies understood his principle perfectly and had understood it for more than three thousand years. The military called it discipline. Techniques varied from army to army; in the Legion it usually meant beating a man to unconsciousness as many times as was necessary to teach him the proper fear of all *sous-officiers*. As dogs were to be conditioned to salivate at the sound of a bell, legionnaires were conditioned to quake at the sight of a *sous-officier*.

"Well," the *sergent-chef* said mockingly, "have you lost your speech, legionnaire?"

"No, sir!" Olive croaked.

"Do you confess to stealing from your fellow legionnaires?"

Olive felt a wildness crawling in his brain. If he did not confess, Ciano would club him to the ground and continue to club him until he did confess or was dead. And if he confessed now, as Ciano wished, it would be the penal battalion and a quick death, if he was lucky.

"I am waiting, legionnaire," Ciano drawled, gripping his ever-present cane with both hands.

Strangely, it did not occur to Olive to fight, so thorough was his conditioning. He had been presented two impossible alternatives, and he had to choose one of them. "I can't confess, *sir!*"

The cane flashed and landed on Olive's cheek. Olive dropped to his knees as though he had been axed. The enraged figure of the *sergent-chef* swam before him. The universe whirled at a sickening rate.

"Get to your feet, legionnaire!"

Olive got to his feet.

"I ask again, legionnaire. Do you confess?"

Guilt or innocence was not the issue. Only the confession mattered. Olive, perhaps because he was still dazed from the first blow, said, "I didn't steal anything, *sir!*" With each word blood poured from the corner of his mouth.

Ciano studied him thoughtfully. Olive told himself, he won't club me again. He believes me. He has to believe me, because it's the truth.

62

Ciano went on looking at him. Olive began to breathe a little easier. He had steeled himself for a second blow from the cane. The blow didn't come. He remained ramrod straight, but inside he relaxed. Then the blow came.

The second blow was more shocking, more shattering than the first. For a time all his senses were tightly wrapped in blackness. He felt himself falling. Then Olive was on his hands and knees, the left side of his face numb. But his brain was on fire.

"Get to your feet, legionnaire," Ciano was saying in a bored tone.

Olive began to know that crushing despair that every legionnaire experienced from time to time. He knew now that nothing, nothing at all, could help him. Ciano was going to have his way. Ciano would report him as a thief, and his own comrades would crucify him with bayonets to an adobe wall. If they didn't kill him. For it was much simpler to lose a comrade than to act contrary to the desires of Sergent-Chef Giuseppe Ciano. Whether or not they had been robbed was not the point and never had been.

Ciano kicked him solidly, expertly, almost absently, and Olive sprawled helplessly in the dirt. "Get to your feet, legionnaire," Ciano repeated monotonously.

Olive got to his feet, somehow. He stood reeling. The *sergent-chef* smiled. Somewhere in the depths of Olive's numbness, in some black corner of his brain the madness beetle, *cafard*, began to stir. Olive felt the beetle's slow awakening, its sluggish kicking. It squirmed and scratched and slowly ascended through the various levels of Olive's consciousness. At last, when it reached the top, it paused and studied the smiling face and figure of iron that was Sergent-Chef Ciano.

Ciano did not notice it at first, the beetle staring steadily at him from behind the glazed, reflective surface of the legionnaire's eyes. He studied the battered and bloody side, the left side, of Olive's face. The secret of the cane was to strike in exactly the same place every time. And yet each blow must be timed so that it was totally unexpected, a bright new shock, a return to the very beginning in the experience of pain. Proper use of the cane was an art, and Sergent-Chef Ciano was its master.

All this was very well; it was the duty of a *sous-officier* to present his officers with perfectly prepared and disciplined troops. But, the experienced and prudent *sous-officier* was always on the alert for the madness beetle. Because Sergent-Chef Ciano overlooked for just a moment this major axiom of the Legion, he died.

Suddenly the impossible, the unthinkable, was happening. Olive was tearing, with all the strength of sudden madness, at Ciano's throat.

The *sergent-chef*, who never once had been totally surprised in battle, was stunned at this attack. This actual physical attack upon the inviolable person of a *sous-officier* of the Legion by a second-class legionnaire! He recovered enough to fight Olive off for a moment. But the legionnaire was a man possessed, also a man doomed, with no possible future. The man who had killed Arabs by the score without a change of expression, stared dumbly as Olive charged again. Even when he allowed Olive to wrench his heavy cane from his huge hands, he seemed capable only of staring in amazement. Olive clubbed him viciously with the cane. Ciano's cheek opened, blood poured, but he did not go down. The incredible truth was no longer to be denied. This dog of a common legionnaire had actually *attacked* him!

Ciano's smile was now a wide, bloody grimace. My dear legionnaire, he thought to himself in a crimson rage, before this fine night is over you'll curse your mother a thousand times for having borne you!

That heavy cane flashed again, falling this time across the *sergent-chef's* close-cropped skull, knocking his gold-trimmed kepi into the dirt and filth of Monterrey. To Ciano's dismay, his iron legs gave way. The cane crashed down again and again. The last thought that flashed through Sergent-Chef Giuseppe Ciano's fiery brain was: *He's going to kill me! This stinking English nobody from the Liverpool gutters is actually going to kill me!*

And that was just what Olive did.

If he had reached up and grasped the sky with his bare hands and pulled it down, he could not have been more amazed or appalled. Ciano the indestructible lay dead, a bloody pulp, at Olive's feet. The madness beetle retreated, trundled back down to some uncharted depth of his mind to rest and wait. He was icily sober and terrified. He did not know the exact penalty for a legionnaire who had killed his chief sergeant, but he was sure that it would not bear dwelling on.

He stood for a moment trying to think. In an instant the *cafard* had left him. He had never been saner, every detail of the scene was stark and hard-edged and all too real. At last he grasped Ciano's feet and pulled him into the darkened alleyway. He recovered the gold-trimmed kepi and tossed it after the body. He darted glances up and down the street, but the area around the cathedral seemed to be deserted. That was something, at least.

Olive tried to think what to do next. One thing was certain, he had fought his last battle, pulled his last tour of duty for *La Légion*. Desertion, always a poor proposition, would be much worse now. Not that he had a choice. The instant he had attacked Ciano he had become a deserter. Anything at all would be immeasurably preferable to turning himself over to the mercies of a Legion court martial.

That first sense of panic, the first terror which had fluttered like swarms of flies over the surface of his skin, began to recede. With Ciano dead, a little of the Legion's conditioning eroded. He breathed deeply and thought, *Take your time. Think about it. And when you've made up your mind, act.*

First of all, he would have to get away from Monterrey. Make for Veracruz perhaps, or some other seaport, and hope to catch a ship which would eventually take him to England.

Not much chance of that with Juárez soldiers and hostile Mexicans all around. The south was out of the question; he would surely run into French forces with orders to shoot him on sight. There was nothing inland but mountains and more Mexicans and hostile Indians. North, like it or not, was his only choice. If he could somehow make it across the Bravo into the United States he might stand a chance.

That settled "where." Next came "how."

First of all he would need money. Quickly he went through the pockets of the dead Ciano and was disgusted but not surprised to find that the sergeant had no money. All right, there was still the deal that he had made with the American bounty hunter. He would have to go through with it, even if it meant tarrying a few hours in Monterrey.

FOUR

Olive's insides fell when he entered the bleak cantina. Trent was not there. A French lieutenant was talking to the spidery little bar-keep. The Mexican listened uninterestedly, shrugging and shaking his head, and after a while the lieutenant left. Olive called for tequila. He needed it. The little man served the drink, gazed at Olive's bloody cheek, but made no comment.

"Look," Olive said in the bar-keep's own language, "there's a pal of mine supposed to be waiting for me here. The Confederate soldier."

The little man looked at him sullenly.

Olive said, "The French officer who just left was looking for the same man."

The bar-keep shrugged. "The French officer likes to ask questions, but he buys no wine. I tell him nothing. It is fair bargain."

Olive grinned one-sidedly and put some silver on the table. "Pour me tequila. Take one for yourself."

The little Mexican took the money for an extra drink but did not pour one for himself. "The one called Trent. The French are very eager to find him."

Olive pushed what was left of the silver toward

the proprietor. He began to worry again. Why was the French Army on Trent's trail? "Do you know where he is?"

Tire little man took the rest of the silver. "You know of a place called Rosa's, facing the Square of Juárez?"

Everybody knew Rosa's, one of the better class of Monterrey taverns.

Rosa herself was a fat, smooth, greedy woman who knew Olive as a common legionnaire who enjoyed drinking and brawling. Rosa had nothing against drinking and brawling so long as all broken furniture was settled for. It added spice to an otherwise dull routine. "Pal of yours upstairs," she told Olive. "In the front room."

"By himself?"

She shrugged. "By himself or not, it's all the same to me. Long as he pays." If she noticed Olive's battered face she didn't think it interesting enough to mention.

Olive had to identify himself and wait for Trent to throw the inside latch before he could get in. The small bedroom was filled with cigar smoke, the windows were shuttered, and the place was stifling. "What happened to you?" was the first thing he said, staring at Olive's face.

Olive only shrugged. He sat on the edge of the bed wishing that he had a drink, but there was no bottle in the room. "I just came from the cantina.

There was a French lieutenant there wondering what had happened to you."

Trent lit a fresh cigar and paced the small room. By lamplight his face looked gray, his eyes quick and wary. "The French regiment. Maybe somebody who had seen me back in Ayersville happened to see me here in Monterrey. Did you find Cameron?"

"I know where he is. That little bartender claims the French are scouting the town for you."

Trent laughed dryly. "I know that very well. Like I told you, the old colonel is partial to Cameron. He threatened to withhold his regiment from French service if his friend was bothered by any more detectives or Union agents. If your legionnaires get their hands on me . . . Well, by the time the military government in Louisiana found out what happened to me, it would be much too late to do anything about it."

Olive was mildly amused to find that he and the detective had at least one thing in common—the Legion would do its best to kill them both. "How did you get here from the cantina, if you knew they were looking for you?"

"Sheer luck!" This was the thing that worried Trent—luck was the one thing that he had trained himself not to depend on. "I was making a visit to the outhouse when the Legion officer came asking about me." He grinned coldly. "That must

70

have posed a problem to that little bartender. He hates Americans and he hates the French, and he couldn't hurt one without helping the other."

Trent fanned his cigar impatiently. "Tell me about Cameron. Where is he?"

"There's something we've got to get settled first. Remember the forty dollars I was to get when I located Cameron for you?"

Trent stopped his pacing and looked at Olive with suspicious eyes. "What about it?"

"It won't be enough," Olive told him. "I need more."

Trent did not like this turn at all. "We made a bargain," he said coldly.

"The bargain's off. I had to kill a legionnaire. A *sous-officier*. There's nothing for me now except desertion. And that will take money."

"I didn't tell you to kill a legionnaire."

But Olive held all the cards, and he knew it. "The way things are going for you, it will take the French about six hours to have you conveniently dead and buried. With money I can get us out of Monterrey."

"I don't leave Monterrey without my prisoner."

Olive sighed but nodded agreement. "All right, we'll make a new bargain. I'll take you to Cameron, and I'll get you through the ring of Legion outposts. Getting back to your own country will be up to you."

"How much?"

Without stopping to think about it, Olive said, "Half the bounty, five hundred dollars."

Trent's eyes seemed to bulge. "You're out of your mind!"

Olive wasn't sure that the detective wasn't right. He had known that Trent would never agree to a price like that. And if he did agree, he would never stay with his word.

After a taut silence, Trent said grimly, "You don't give a man much choice, do you?"

Olive did not miss the ominous, unspoken threat that lay behind the words. "That's right. Neither of us has much choice. Comrades of circumstance, as they say."

For several seconds Trent gazed coldly, levelly at the legionnaire, like a professional hangman measuring his man for the drop. "First, before anything else, I must be taken to Cameron."

Olive grinned his false grin. "Fair enough. I intend to earn my way, and my half of the bounty. Besides, they've got him nested away in a church, and getting him out without making an unholy do might take a bit of handling."

Trent ground his teeth and Olive saw a muscle jumping at the corner of his jaw. At last he said, "We might as well get on with it."

"My thoughts exactly," Olive said, with only a hint of irony.

Rosa met them at the bottom of the stairs and Olive good-naturedly patted her smooth face.

"Rosa, my love, it is just possible that some French gentlemen will come asking certain questions concerning myself or Señor Trent. You might tell them that, yes, we were here, and that you just happened to overhear one of us say that our immediate destination is Veracruz." He held out a hand and said to Trent in English, "Give me one of the gold pieces, and don't argue."

The detective did as he was told, but angrily and grudgingly. Olive placed the gold piece in Rosa's smooth pink palm. Rosa beamed. "I understand perfectly. *Adiós*, legionnaire. *Adiós*, *señor*."

When they were outside, Trent demanded, "Can that woman be trusted?"

"I don't know," Olive confessed, "but it's worth a gamble, considering our lives may depend on it."

They hurried toward the stables which Rosa kept for the convenience of her patrons. A young stable hand saddled Trent's animal. As usual, Trent had kept his expensive Henry with him; only at the last moment did he shove it into the saddle boot. "Where is the church?"

"I'll show you."

Trent led the horse. Olive, anonymous in his uniform, scouted ahead through the twisting alleys. At last they were standing before that Gothic mountain of stone and stained glass which was Saint Mark.

"See that narrow window just below the bell tower? That's where your man is."

Trent gazed at it for several seconds. "How do we get to it?"

"The church isn't locked. But what do we do about Cameron when we find him? 'Dead or alive,' it said on the poster."

"Alive," Trent said. "If possible."

Olive shrugged. "I'll need some sort of weapon."

"The Henry's the only weapon I have." Then he had a second thought and said, "I do have a knife."

But it was a great deal more than merely a knife. Trent, who knew little of Texas or Texans, had been dimly amused by the size and weight of that full-tanged blade. He had bought it to use as a serviceable camp tool more than a weapon. But Olive recognized it instantly for what it was—an instrument of death. He handled it with respect and affection, feeling its balance and palm-fitted haft. The ghost of Colonel Bowie must have smiled to see a man who so admired his handiwork.

Cameron could not sleep. He paced the floor of his cell, as impatient as a prisoner on the last day of his sentence. A pale, sickly light lay on Monterrey, but the night air smelled of freedom. He paused by the slit of a window and sniffed at the night like a caged hound. The colonel, he decided, had the right idea after all. Just to be with the regiment again was an end in itself. To be among old comrades, trusted friends. After all, most of their adult lives had been devoted to soldiering; it was natural for a man to want to return to the thing he knew.

He didn't actually believe it, but there was no alternative left to him. "Make do" was the old soldier's slogan.

Accept your situation and make the most of it.

He wondered what time it was. Three or four hours must have passed since the colonel's visit—that would make it close to midnight. If Montfort's expectations became realities and the regiment actually did receive its marching orders, Cameron might expect word at any time. For this reason he was not surprised to hear the resounding tramp of boots in the corridor outside his cell.

There was a solid one-two tap on the door. It was not Montfort's knock, but then Cameron had not expected the colonel himself at this time of night. A businesslike voice was muffled by the heavy oak door. "Captain Cameron?"

Cameron made for the door but hesitated before throwing the bolt. "Who is it?"

"Corporal Olive, sir."

"What's your outfit?"

"Headquarters. Detached service, sir." Cameron

knew no Corporal Olive, but there was nothing unusual in that. In recent months many obscure privates had been promoted to non-coms and even officers. And soldiers were often shifted from one outfit to another in the Confederacy's woefully undermanned regiments. "I'm on Colonel Montfort's personal orders, sir," the voice said with just the right blend of respect and impatience.

Cameron threw the bolt and opened the door. At the last moment it occurred to him that Corporal Olive spoke in a clipped accent which, while military, was disturbingly un-Southern.

But by then it was much too late to ponder this inconsistency. Pale light from the window fell across Olive's grinning face. A Foreign Legionnaire! Cameron was surprised but not unnecessarily disturbed—after all, Montfort's regiment and the French forces would soon be fighting on the same side. It was possible, if not very probable, that a Legion non-com might serve temporarily with the Americans in a liaison capacity.

But these thoughts passed so quickly through Cameron's mind that he was hardly aware of them at all. In his hand Legionnaire Olive held the perfect antidote to optimism.

The hand with the bowie knife whipped through the pale swath of light so that the tilted point hooked just beneath Cameron's chin.

"Don't move," Olive told him quietly. "Don't make a sound. Don't even breathe."

Cameron froze. After four years of war he did not have to prove his courage. And he was no fool. No weapon in his extended experience had quite the authority of a well-honed, seven-pound fighting knife. Neither saber nor rifle, pistol nor bayonet commanded respect as positively as did Jim Bowie's iron mistress.

The hand that held the knife was completely steady. The steel point had opened a small wound and Cameron could feel the warm blood trickling down his neck. His blood. He tried not to think about that.

His mind raced but did not go out of control. He measured the legionnaire with one quick glance and correctly judged him to be a conscienceless killer but probably not an indiscriminate one. There was a reason for his being here—a definite and profitable reason. And the reason was not to kill, else Cameron would have died the instant he had opened the door.

Cameron tried to speak, but he could not open his mouth without driving the knife point deeper into his throat. The legionnaire spoke to someone back in the dark corridor.

"Looks like our man, all right, but I'd like to see him in some better light. Wouldn't do to start making mistakes at this point."

A face appeared over the legionnaire's left

shoulder. "Move him inside and close the door. Careful now, don't let him pull any tricks."

Olive nodded to Cameron. "Two steps back. Easy does it, Captain."

Cameron and Olive moved together into the cell. The second man sidled around them and closed the door. Then he struck a sulphur match and studied Cameron's taut features in the harsh light. He smiled, very faintly. "Wardson Lee Cameron, under the authority of the office of the United States marshal, district of Southern Louisiana, I hereby arrest you for the murder of the mayor of Ayersville, Louisiana, one Stuart Jeffers, and for other crimes against the government of"—he paused with an air of extreme satisfaction—"but I'm sure you understand all this, don't you, Cameron?"

At a sign from the detective, Olive eased the pressure of the knife enough to allow Cameron to speak.

Cameron breathed deeply, struggling to rein in his anger. "I see," he said at last. "You'd be the detective called Trent."

Trent bowed mockingly. "At your service, Captain. In a manner of speaking."

"And this legionnaire?"

"An . . . associate, you might say."

"A deserter. You're pushing your luck, Trent. Do you know what happens to deserters in the Legion? And to those who help them?"

The detective shrugged, interested only in the successful conclusion of his assignment. Methodically, Trent searched Cameron while Olive held him immobile with the knife. Near the window Trent found a small tallow candle and lit it. He went through Cameron's war bag with the thoroughness of a bank examiner, thoughtfully inspecting each personal item, paper, or letter. With special interest he examined a Prescott navy revolver, manufactured some five years earlier at Worcester, Massachusetts, and no doubt taken from a fallen or captured Union officer.

"A bonus," Trent said, shoving the revolver into the legionnaire's waistband. "A reasonably decent handgun and two boxes of rim-fire cartridges to go with it."

Olive accepted the revolver and ammunition but only grunted. He would much rather have had a serviceable rifle. "What else did you find in his kit?" he asked, still holding Cameron motionless with the knife.

"A few personal letters and papers," Trent said. "Enough to prove who he is, in case I have to deliver a body instead of a man. That"— he smiled at Cameron—"will be up to you, Captain."

Cameron choked down a hot reply. For the present it was Trent's game and would have to be played by Trent's rules. The detective discarded what he could not use and pocketed the letters and other papers, among them a military pardon that Washington had routinely issued to Confederate officers.

At first Cameron was vaguely comforted by the knowledge that it was a long, long way from Monterrey to Ayersville, Louisiana, and that many opportunities for escape were sure to occur along the way. Then he realized that actually Trent had only to get him across the border of Texas and into the hands of some carpetbagger official. The Army of Occupation would take over from there, and with pleasure.

"I don't know about you," Olive was saying without moving his steady gaze from Cameron's face, "but I'd be just as pleased to see the last of this part of Mexico."

Trent agreed completely. He moved to the door and was about to open it when they heard the clop-clop of loose-fitting sandals in the corridor.

Olive looked thoughtful. "Keep an eye on this one," he said to Trent. He kept his knife steady until the detective had the muzzle of his Henry firmly against Cameron's chest. Then Olive moved to the door. Silently, he drew the bolt and stepped into the corridor.

"Father," he said quietly.

Only at that moment did Cameron begin to guess what the legionnaire had in mind. He started to yell, despite the pressure of the rifle against his chest. But Trent had anticipated him. With an expertness that was surprising, the detective savagely clubbed Cameron with the walnut stock of his rifle.

There was a brilliant explosion inside Cameron's head. His stomach raced to his throat and suddenly he found himself on all fours on the stone floor of the cell. He clung firmly to the frayed edge of consciousness, but beyond that he was incapable of thought or action.

"Was it necessary to kill him?" Trent was asking. He sounded mildly irritated.

"The fewer witnesses we leave behind, the better for both of us," Olive said indifferently.

Again the clipped preciseness of Olive's speech sounded an alien note in Cameron's ears. Still on his hands and knees, Cameron raised his head. Blood from a scalp wound trickled down his forehead and into his eyes. With great effort he raised himself to his haunches and wiped his eyes.

Trent was directly in front of him, holding the rifle less than an inch from Cameron's heart. "The more I think about it, Captain," the detective said blandly, "the prospect of taking you in dead becomes less and less distasteful. So don't tempt me by doing something foolish."

Near the door the legionnaire was pulling the priest's rough-textured cassock over his head.

"How do I look?" he asked, smoothing the robe over his baggy trousers and covering his head with the hood.

"Not much like a holy father," the detective said sourly, "with those marching boots on."

Olive swore under his breath. Then he left the room for a few minutes and came back with the priest's sandals. He sat on the floor and, with a look of great relief, tugged the hard, unyielding Legion boots from his bare feet. His feet were covered with sores and blisters and scars of old blisters, as were the feet of all legionnaires. He stretched his toes luxuriously and at last pulled on the thonged sandals. He made a bundle of his Legion greatcoat and boots and tucked it under his arm.

As for the murder of the priest, he did not give it another thought. In the eyes of the Legion, the death of a holy man was less than nothing when compared to the murder of a *sous-officier*.

Sometimes, to a man with years of war behind him, the death of a single man can be more shattering than the deaths of hundreds. This was the way Olive's indifferent murder of the priest had affected Ward Cameron.

Stunned, Cameron moved obediently when Trent gestured toward the door. Olive was the first to step quickly into the dark corridor. By the last light of the flickering candle Cameron saw the neat rent and bright stain in the back of the cassock. This was somehow more chilling than all the mangled bodies and rivers of blood that he had seen during the war.

The huddled body of the priest lay on the stone floor of the corridor, but Olive did not give it a glance. "Hurry along," the legionnaire snapped. "I don't intend to spend the rest of the night in this place."

Now Trent was leading the way down the twisting stairway and the legionnaire was behind Cameron, holding the keen point of the fighting knife in the small of his back.

They reached the landing and moved quietly toward the entrance of the cathedral. For a moment they paused beneath the great Gothic arch. Trent scouted for a moment and then returned.

"Seems to be clear," he told the legionnaire. "It's up to you to see us through the Legion out-posts."

"That's the easy part. But I told you it would be expensive."

From the sudden electricity in the air, Cameron sensed that the subject of money had been dis-cussed before. Grudgingly, the detective counted three gold pieces into Olive's palm.

The legionnaire grinned. "There's one more thing."

The detective looked sharply. "What?"

"Horses. We need two horses, beside that roan of yours."

"Impossible," Trent snorted. "Except for the nags that the Confederates rode from Texas, there probably isn't a saddle animal in Monterrey."

"As a matter of fact," Olive said, "those were just the animals I had in mind." Suddenly his voice grew hard. "You didn't think I would let myself be caught afoot while you rode off on a good horse, armed with a good rifle, with a thousand-dollar prisoner in tow?"

Trent's face went red. His neck began to swell. He reminded Cameron of a pig bladder filled with air and left in the hot sun to explode. Cameron watched in fascination this brief, violent battle of wills. And when, after a moment, the battle was over, he realized that a balance of strength had subtly shifted in favor of the legionnaire.

The Confederate camp was on a plain just south of Monterrey. A feeling of nostalgia and sadness came over Cameron when he saw that shapeless cluster of dog tents and other make-do shelters, the horses huffing, stamping, dozing at the picket lines. There were scattered fires throughout the camp where men huddled together, talking of times long gone and friends long dead. There were always those who could not sleep before a battle, and Cameron could sense an air of expectancy, a nervousness that always swept ahead of a major action. Then Cameron saw how spent they were, how gaunt and empty and hollow eyed. These men without home or country or cause—and Cameron himself was one of them.

Cameron and Olive lay on a rocky grade looking down on the camp. They could see the sentries plodding blindly up and down and smell the wild perfume of burning sage. They saw Trent striding with a kind of unconscious arrogance toward the camp, heard the sentry challenge him sleepily. Trent and the sentry talked for a moment and then the detective moved on toward the picket lines.

"He's going to make it!" Olive said, shaking his head in wonder. "Lord, what an army! I'm not surprised you lost the war."

The wonder of it was that they lasted so long, not that they had lost. But Cameron had no wish to discuss the war with a Foreign Legionnaire.

Olive, with the point of the bowie knife still at Cameron's throat, made his observations with a coldly objective eye. "If that sentry was a legionnaire," he said grimly, "his future wouldn't be a thing you'd care to think about. Hung by his thumbs and beat unconscious would be the very best he could expect. Most likely he would find himself crucified to a barrack wall."

Cameron turned his head carefully and looked at Olive's face. Obviously the man hated the Legion with a passion that could not be described, and at the same time he was proud of having been a legionnaire. Cameron was surprised to discover that this was a kind of contradiction that he could understand.

Down in the camp Trent had confidently taken a horse from the picket line and was beginning to get it saddled.

"How long have you been in the Legion?" Cameron asked.

"Seven years. Started my second enlistment before the regiment left Algeria."

Cameron was truly curious. "Deserting the Legion must be a simple matter. You seem to be taking it calmly enough."

Olive shot him a pitying look. "Deserting the Legion is practically impossible. Not one in a hundred ever makes it."

"Then why . . . ? Is the bounty money worth all that risk?"

"A thousand American dollars—that's more money than I can rightly think about at one time!" Olive laughed dryly. "But it's not worth deserting the Legion for. A legionnaire deserts only when he has no other choice."

A thousand American dollars he had said. Did that mean that Olive had no intention of dividing the reward with Trent? It was an interesting thought. And, Cameron realized, it might be his one hope of escape.

"Look at that!" Olive said in amazement.

But Cameron couldn't look until the legionnaire eased the pressure of the knife. Olive obliged with a wry grin. "When I said two horses," he said with a trace of awe, "I thought it would be impossible. But have a look!"

Cameron looked. Amazingly enough, Trent was unhurriedly riding one animal away from the camp and leading a second.

"Our Mr. Trent," Olive said grudgingly, "has got more spunk than I gave him credit for."

"I'm afraid," Cameron said with a certain dryness, "that neither of us has appreciated Mr. Trent's resourcefulness."

The legionnaire didn't know just how resourceful the detective had been. Cameron immediately recognized the animal that Trent was riding as his own, a war-weary dun that he had raised from a colt. The horse that Trent was leading was a coal-black gelding, Colonel Montfort's favorite saddle animal since the early days of the war.

Every man in the regiment must have known that black. But no one tried to stop Trent. No one shouted or even questioned. He simply rode away, and the men huddling about the campfires, communing with ghosts, did not even bother to look up.

Trent rode directly toward the heart of the town. "Let's go," Olive said shortly. They crawled down the slope and made for the weed-grown gully where they had left Trent's roan, Cameron always half a step ahead of the legionnaire, the knife point a constant warning against his side. They made a strange pair in the moonlight—the Confederate officer and the hooded legionnaire with gray cassock flapping about his legs. His Legion greatcoat had long since been discarded.

Trent was waiting for them beside an old adobe corral, out of sight of the camp. "I've got to hand it to you," Olive said in frank admiration. "That was a neater job than anybody had a right to expect. What did you say to that sentry?"

"I told him the colonel was ready to take Captain Cameron out of hiding, and they wanted their horses. It sounded reasonable enough; the whole regiment knows they'll be pulling out in a matter of hours."

His loose sandals flapping, Olive clopped through the silent streets of Monterrey. Trent rode alongside on his own roan, leading the black. Cameron, with the detective's revolver at his back, was astride the dun. Near the center of the town they saw a roving French patrol enter the street and come toward them. With new firmness, Trent pushed the muzzle into Cameron's back. "I hope you understand, Captain, that I will not hesitate to kill you instantly if you make an improper move or sound."

Trent, with the French officials already looking

for him, had nothing to lose. But Olive, whose situation was even more desperate, fell back a pace to make another point.

"Remember the dead priest, Captain? Nobody saw me or Trent go into the church. And nobody saw us come out. Who do you think the French will be looking for when the murder is discovered?"

Cameron went cold. It hadn't occurred to him that Captain Wardson Lee Cameron himself was the most logical murder suspect.

Olive saw the look of shock on Cameron's face. In that dark opening of the cassock hood, the legionnaire was smiling. Then he clopped ahead quickly to meet the patrol.

The patrol consisted of six legionnaires and a pink-cheeked lieutenant. The lieutenant gave the order to halt and order arms. He then advanced to meet the "priest," his puzzled glance moving from the cassocked figure to the two mounted men in Confederate uniforms.

"You must know, Father," the young officer chided gently, "the hour is very late, much past curfew. I'm afraid I must . . ."

Olive raised a hand and managed to sound suitably pompous. "The law of man, my son, not of God."

"Nevertheless, Father, I have my duty. . . ."

"And I mine," Olive interrupted with gentle determination. Cameron was so intrigued by the legionnaire's performance that he could almost forget the boring threat of the pistol in his back. "My son, at this very moment a man lies sick and dying with the plague—would you deny last rites to a dying man?"

Involuntarily, the lieutenant took a step back at the mention of plague. He was not at all sure just how such a situation should be handled. "I understand," he said, although he understood nothing at all. "But who are these American soldiers, Father, and why are they with you?"

Olive again raised a hand, as if in benediction. "The poor man who lies dying is a comrade of these brave soldiers who, I have heard, will march tomorrow to join your Marshal Bazaine. These men are prepared to fight, and perhaps die, for the further glory of France. I cannot believe that a dedicated Frenchman would interfere. . . ."

The young officer threw up his arms with a groan. He knew very well how powerful the priesthood, in its own quiet way, could be. "Very well, Father . . ." He left the sentence unfinished and resignedly waved the patrol on.

Trent chuckled as they moved to the north. "That was some act. You had that pup eating right out of your hand."

Olive was not moved. "We were lucky," he said darkly. "I don't like to think how it would have gone if a sergeant, or even a corporal, had been in charge of the patrol. When we reach the outposts there'll be no pink-cheeked lieutenants to swallow foolish stories."

"You have the bribe money," Trent reminded him.

"Yes. And let us hope that the outpost sentries are greedy."

They moved on to the outer fringe of the town. When they neared the first sentry box Olive hesitated, thought furiously for a moment, and then skinned quickly out of the bulky cassock. "Lay behind a few paces," he told the detective, "and make sure the captain doesn't do something foolish. It would only mean the sentry's death, as well as his own."

"*Halte-la!*" the sentry snapped as Olive came toward him out of the darkness.

Olive recognized the voice; it belonged to one Legionnaire First Class Martini, a moody little Sicilian whose single ambition in life was to become a *sous-officier*. Olive felt his hopes sinking. But he called good-naturedly, "It is Legionnaire Olive of First Company. You know me well enough."

Martini was immediately suspicious. "What is it?" He came forward a few steps, his heavy Belgian rifle at the ready. "What do you want?"

Olive laughed. "I'm a soldier of France, Martini. The Legion gives me what I need; why should I want anything?"

Martini was not amused. When the recruiting

91

officer had accepted his first enlistment and told him that for the next five years the Legion would be his home, it had been the simple truth. "I am on duty," he said shortly. "Go to your squad, Olive, before you get us both in trouble."

"I won't get us in trouble, Martini. But it might be that I can make you a rich man. Listen . . ." He moved forward again, moving casually toward the sentry's bayonet. It was taking a chance, for Martini was one of those rare men who was perfectly satisfied with the Legion and never dreamed of anything better. But at the same time he was a Sicilian, and anything smacking of wealth was hypnotic to him. "Are you drunk, Olive? Or is that *cafard* talking?"

Olive held out a gold piece. "Does this look like wine or madness beetles, Martini? This is American gold. It's yours, Martini. You can have it."

The legionnaire stared at the small disk of yellow. Even in the pale night light it gleamed richly. "What are you up to, Olive?"

"An errand of mercy, you might say," Olive told him. "I have two friends with me, American soldiers who tomorrow will be marching to meet Bazaine. But tonight—you know how it is, Martini. Before an action a man does not want the company of other men. It just happens that I know two ladies—not these Monterrey hags, mind you, but ladies—gentle enough to please even these American officers. Unfortunately, the ladies live up the street a short distance. . . ."

Martini shook his head. "Impossible. Return to your squad, Olive, and tell your Americans to return to theirs."

Olive sighed to himself. "Don't you understand, Martini? The gold is yours. All you have to do is let us pass."

Martini stared at the gold with lust. But with such men, *A moi La Légion* translated literally. Olive sighed again, this time aloud. "Too bad," he said sadly. "Too bad."

Martini, thinking that he referred to the loss of the gold, agreed with mind and heart. But his soul was the Legion's. He managed to shrug. He dragged his gaze from the gold piece. "Now go away from here, Olive."

". . . Very well." With infinite weariness, Olive turned. "*Bon soir*, Martini."

"*Bon soir*," the sentry said impatiently. He smartly about-faced, preparing to return to his post.

Olive wheeled. Colonel Bowie's iron mistress gleamed dully in the legionnaire's hand. There was hardly a sound. A groan, a muffled thud, as Martini sank to the dust. A small clatter as his rifle fell from his hands. "Too bad," Olive said again, "that you couldn't have listened to reason, Martini."

FIVE

Sunup saw the trip far north of Monterrey, but not far enough to suit Legionnaire William Olive. Trent was all for stopping to rest the horses, as well as themselves—but the detective had never seen a deserter spread-eagled in the broiling sun with his mouth filled with salt. Ward Cameron had nothing to say about it one way or the other.

By midday they had covered half the distance to Laredo and even Olive was ready to rest. In *la cavalerie à pied*, the "foot cavalry," as the Legion was sometimes called, he was accustomed to marching forty miles a day, and he could sit the hump of a lurching camel when he was too drunk to stand, but with horses he had had little experience. The private soldier of France traveled on his own feet. Only officers rode horses. Such animals, Olive had been taught, definitely were not for the likes of dock workers and second-class legionnaires—and at this moment he believed it thoroughly.

His body ached from unaccustomed strains and pressures, and like the others he was hungry and sweated dry. "This will do," he said at last, when they came upon a cactus-veiled gully with a gyp water trickle at the bottom. The bitterness of the water caused Trent to recoil with a curse, and the horses drank only a little. But Olive and Cameron, old soldiers that they were, drank not to slake their thirst but to replace moisture that had been sweated out of their bodies.

They sat with their backs against the clay banks of the gully. The regiment, Cameron thought, would be well on its way to meet Bazaine by this time. Colonel Montfort would be puzzled and perhaps hurt at his captain's disappearance. But he would not delay the movement of the regiment because of one man.

Cameron glanced cautiously at his captors. Trent was beginning to show the strain of the forced march. Exhaustion and thirst had made his nerves raw, and suspicion of his partner would not allow him to rest. Also, his stomach was not used to camp food and gyp water—there was a certain paleness about his mouth and feverishness in his eyes.

In Olive's eyes there was only hunger—the kind of hunger that a thousand-dollar bounty could cause.

Suddenly Olive lurched to his feet. "Enough of this," he said impatiently. "How far do we have to go?"

"Too far," Trent said wearily, "to go any farther in daylight. Besides, the horses need to rest."

"The horses can rest when we're out of Mexico."

Cameron was looking from one to the other

and smiling faintly. Olive saw him and his eyes turned angry. "Captain, I wouldn't say that you have a great deal to smile about."

"I was just thinking," Cameron drawled. "We're in Juárez country now. From here to the border his peon army will control all the main roads and trails. I wouldn't much like to be caught by them, especially if I was wearing a French uniform."

Olive looked at him with slitted eyes.

"I agree," Trent said. "It's better to wait for night before going on. We don't have to make for Laredo. Carrizo, maybe. There are good crossings there."

Surprisingly, Olive did not object. "Maybe you're right." He shrugged. "Not likely the Legion is after me yet. And even if it is, there are orders from Paris, I've heard, that forbid any French action north of Monterrey." He didn't add that orders from Paris had a way of getting lost when they tended to interfere with Legion discipline.

An uneasy quiet settled over the gully. They had nothing to eat, and nothing to drink but the gyp water. Trent relaxed against the clay bank and his eyes slowly closed. Olive said, "Might as well make the best of things, Captain." He got up and bound Cameron's feet, as well as his hands. "There, now we can all get a little rest."

Secure in the knowledge that his prisoner could not escape, Olive found a patch of shade opposite

Cameron. He closed his eyes and seemed to be asleep. The Mexican sun seared the barren landscape; heat waves rose like smoke from that land of rock and cactus until Cameron could almost believe that the earth itself was on fire. For one violent moment he strained at the hemp rope that bound his wrists, but the legionnaire had done his work well.

Cameron lay back against the dirt wall, sweat running into his eyes. He tried to be calm. Save your strength, he thought. He could see the wall of distrust growing between his two captors. Sooner or later the break would be complete. That would be the time to act.

But he hadn't expected the break so soon, and he hadn't expected it to be so violent. The single rifleshot rolled like thunder between the close walls of the gully.

Cameron had been dozing, making himself as comfortable as possible. The explosion shocked him instantly alert. He saw Legionnaire William Olive lower the muzzle of the detective's Henry and stroke it affectionately. "A wonderful rifle," he said in a tone of total detachment. "A truly beautiful weapon." He glanced at Cameron. "Can you imagine what a company of legionnaires would be capable of, equipped with rifles like this?"

But Cameron was staring at Trent—or the dead, still thing that had *been* Trent.

The detective lay arched backward on the clay floor of the gully as if he had frozen in the midst of a convulsion. He had been shot in the back of the head. The hole near the base of the skull was relatively small and neat, but Cameron was just as glad that the detective had fallen facing in the opposite direction and that what had once been a face could not be seen.

Olive glanced at the corpse and then turned back to Cameron. "Why do you look surprised, Captain? This is exactly what you planned from the beginning. I could see it. You knew that men like me and Trent would never be satisfied with half a bounty. That's why you've come along so peaceful-like—waiting for one of us to kill the other. Now your chances of escaping are twice as good as they were a few minutes ago. Am I right?"

Cameron stared. His mouth was so dry that he didn't trust himself to speak.

Olive laughed. "Don't believe it, Captain. I'm not your Mr. Trent. In the Legion a man develops a strong stomach. The first trick you try, I'll take you back a corpse, even if I have to fight buzzards for you. I'll take you back and I'll collect that bounty—those are two things in this uncertain world that you can believe in."

There was not the slightest doubt in Cameron's mind that Olive meant every word he said. The legionnaire looked again at the dead man and shook his head in mock sadness. "Ignorance like your Mr. Trent's is more to be pitied than scorned. He should have known that a deserter can't go about forever in his old uniform. And seeing that we're near the same size, he should have guessed, really . . ."

"You killed him," Cameron said in a strangely thin voice, "just to get his clothing?"

"And the bounty, Captain. The *full* bounty."

With a practiced touch, Olive emptied the detective's pockets. He spent several minutes studying the packet of wanted posters and arrest warrants.

"Captain," he said cheerfully, "I can see a whole new world opening up for me! It's just the thing the Legion has trained me for, and I never realized it until now. Bounty hunting!" He spoke the word as if it were music. "Did you know," he went on, "that I've tracked down Bedouin renegades over fifty miles of wind-swept sand? And pirates over more miles of naked rock and wasteland than I like to think about?" He broke off and grinned. "It's funny, in a way. All these years I've cursed the Legion in a dozen different tongues—and all the time the Legion was preparing William Olive to be a rich man!"

Olive stripped the dead detective and tried on the Confederate uniform. He was as pleased as a boy with his first long pants. He was especially taken with Trent's boots. After years of marching in iron-hard Legion footgear, the soft leather of these expensive, handmade boots were like caresses to his battered feet.

"Wonderful!" he said in amazement, marching up and down the gully alongside the corpse of their former owner. "I wonder if he had them made in London." He looked at Cameron's expression of disgust and laughed. "I don't understand you, Captain. Why should you worry over what's happened to Trent? He was no friend of yours."

"He was a man."

Olive was truly puzzled. "Let me ask you something, Captain—how many men have you killed?"

Cameron was tempted to mention the necessities of war. But now that it was over, he was no longer so sure what was necessary and what wasn't. Olive chuckled in his dry, humorless way.

They rested till sun up and then left the gully, Olive riding the roan and leading the black. He realized that there was some slight danger that someone would recognize the black as Colonel Montfort's personal animal—but horses were valuable and Olive did not intend to let this one go. Cameron rode the dun, his hands tied to the saddle horn.

Olive was in a cheerful mood. He was just

beginning to taste his freedom from Legion discipline and anticipate the riches that awaited him in that incredible country of the United States. He had no feelings at all toward his prisoner. If Cameron behaved himself, Olive had nothing against letting him live. If not . . . Dead or alive, it didn't really matter.

Only a growling hunger prevented the legionnaire's satisfaction from being complete, and even in hunger he found a wry kind of humor. This was something else that the Legion had taught him—how to bear hunger, along with a thousand other miseries great and small.

They crossed the Bravo somewhere below Carrizo, and Olive, in spite of himself, felt disappointment. It was reasonable to assume that one bank of a river should be much the same as the other, but somehow he had expected something more of Texas than sterile expanses of thornbush and prickly pear. And wild longhorn cattle as dangerous as tigers.

Cameron was watching him expectantly, wondering what his first move would be. Olive himself was undecided. His first inclination was to make straight for Carrizo and exchange his prisoner for cash. But the American war had been over such a short time he couldn't be sure that occupying forces had reached this far south. Riding blindly into a southern town with a Confederate soldier as his prisoner could very possibly be a mistake that no bounty hunter would live to make twice.

"Reconnoiter," he said, thinking aloud. He motioned for Cameron to continue on to the north.

The morning passed. The dazzling sun sweated them dry, left them empty-gutted and dizzy. At every brush-grown hill Olive expected to see a town, or at least a house, on the other side. What they saw was more brush, and wild cattle that ran like deer. Olive was beginning to believe that Texans were a myth and that Texas itself was one great empty desert.

At last they raised a squat adobe hut on a far slope. Olive regarded it thoughtfully, always keeping one eye on his prisoner. "It's not much to look at," he said. "Who would try to live in a place like this?"

Cameron shrugged. "Cow hunters. Before the war they made a kind of living rounding up cattle, driving them to the Gulf and shipping them to New Orleans. But nowadays not many in New Orleans can afford beef. Hide and tallow, that's about all these cattle are good for now."

"Can't be much of a business," Olive decided. "The place looks deserted." They approached cautiously. After a while they sighted the scaffold and pully of a well. "Anyway, maybe there's some water to wet ourselves with."

As they came closer they noted the brush

corral with one side torn away. And a mound of raw red dirt not far from the corral, and a second mound up the slope a short distance from the hut. Olive reined up, regarding the scene with suspicious eyes. "What do you make of it, Captain?"

"Same as you," Cameron told him. "Thieves. Maybe just a band of war scavengers. Broke open the brush corral and took the stock. Probably killed the cow hunter that lived here."

They rode up to the hut's gravelly dooryard. Olive dismounted and tied the horses to the well scaffold. He quickly lowered the bucket and Cameron heard the musical splash as it reached bottom.

"Ah-h-h!" the legionnaire said with enormous satisfaction as he drank directly from the bucket. "Better than wine, almost!" What he didn't drink he poured over his head. Cameron's stomach constricted when he saw the clear water soak into the dry earth.

Kate Barringer had watched them riding down the long slope toward the adobe. From the hut's single window she had followed their progress through thorny thickets and around rugged outcroppings. She had watched them with the chill impersonality of a lizard watching a fly. In her mind there was only one thought, one problem. As soon as they came close enough she had to decide which of these two men she would kill. Her only weapon was the unwieldy musket that Karl had brought with him from Louisiana before the war. After one shot, she knew that she would not have time to reload for another.

Over the sightless barrel of the musket she watched their progress. The men wore odd bits and pieces of Confederate uniforms, but that meant nothing. Texas had her turncoats, as did every other state in the Confederacy. The scavengers of war were everywhere.

For a little while she lost sight of them as they circled what was left of the brush corral. Then she heard the horses crossing the yard and one of the men splashing and gurgling at the well. She moved to the other side of the hut where she could stand in the deep shadow and observe them. The one at the well, she noted, was heavily armed. In his waistband there was a revolver and a heavy fighting knife. A repeating rifle rested nearby against the well scaffolding.

Strangely, the second man, who remained mounted, did not seem to be armed. From where she stood she could not see the ropes on Cameron's wrists.

Her problem had solved itself. Obviously, the armed man was the one she must kill first. Then, if all went well, she would dash to the well, snatch the stranger's rifle and kill the man who remained mounted. It never once occurred to her that it might not be necessary to kill them and anyone else who approached her adobe.

Kate Barringer held the long barrel steady by pressing the muzzle against the door frame. With not a tremor of emotion she aimed very carefully at the stranger's heart. The musket was quite old and unreliable so everything had to be done just right. When the stranger's chest was directly in line with the barrel, she slowly squeezed the trigger, the way Karl had taught her.

The explosion was like thunder. The great flash of fire was blinding, and the boiling black powder smoke was stifling inside the hut.

In the midst of the confusion she heard the man yelp in pain. She had hit him. He was down. Kate dashed from the hut and raced toward the well where the rifle was. At the last moment she saw that her shot had not been a complete success after all. The man was on the ground with a bloody shoulder, but he was far from death.

In an instant Olive's first sensation of shock and pain became coldly determined anger. He saw the woman flinging away the useless musket, and he smiled grimly. The legionnaire, with his good right hand, grabbed for the revolver in his waistband. That Kate Barringer was a woman—a young and reasonably handsome woman at that—did not figure at all in Olive's thoughts.

Cameron heard himself shouting hoarsely. No one paid the slightest attention. The dun, frightened, was shying and side-stepping nervously. In the meantime Olive had leveled his revolver and was ready to fire point-blank at the woman.

Cameron kicked the dun savagely with his spurred heels. Four years of wartime cavalry training came to his aid. He kneed the animal sharply to the right. The dun's flank struck Olive's shoulder, sent him spinning, and knocked the revolver from his hand.

For a moment the woman stood and stared, her eyes curiously blank. Then she darted for the revolver, still intent on killing Olive. By the time Cameron could knee the dun around again she had the weapon in her hand. She held the muzzle not more than a foot from Olive's head and her finger was tight on the trigger.

Cameron heard himself saying, "No!" He didn't know why he said it. Olive with a .36 caliber bullet in his brain would have made life much simpler. But he did say it, and somehow the words reached the woman through her icy calm.

Olive's eyes were dark with rage, but he was sweating profusely and knew that death was only an instant away. Then, at the last split second, the woman's finger held steady on the trigger.

Olive was about to grin when Cameron said, "Put both hands behind your back and don't move." Then, to the woman, "If he doesn't do as I say, kill him."

Olive was sweating again. In the past few hours he had become accustomed to the idea of William Olive, a man with a future, and a very pleasant future at that. His indifference to death, which was as much a part of the Legion as the white kepi and puggree, had been diluted by the prospect of future riches. He glanced at Cameron and then at the woman. Finally he put his right hand behind his back. His left hand felt cold and was glistening with blood. "I can't move this one," he said bitterly.

Cameron nodded to the woman. "Take the knife from his waistband and cut my hands free."

It occurred to her that both men were now at her mercy. One at her feet, helpless, the other with his hands tied to his saddle. She didn't wonder at the strangeness of the situation, she accepted it as it was.

A cold hand seemed to lie on Cameron's back. He could almost see the thoughts moving through the woman's mind. First she would shoot Olive—no, *first* she would take the knife. Then she would approach the mounted man, as if to cut him free. Clearly the mounted man had to be killed first, else he might escape. With that taken care of, she could then kill the man on the ground who was unarmed and helpless.

She looked with eerie emptiness into Olive's eyes as she reached for the knife. The muzzle of the revolver was pressed against his chest so that he did not dare move. But a little ripple of nerves went up his back when he studied the blankness of her expression.

Cafard. He had seen the madness beetle too many times to mistake it for anything else.

It flashed through Cameron's mind that he still had a chance. He could kick the dun and make a run for it. It would take a sharpshooter to pick a man from a running horse with a revolver, and he doubted that this woman was that much of a marksman.

But he did not make the move. He could not say exactly why, except that he had seen women like her before, sometimes standing in the charred wreckage of their homes, or in burned-out fields, or beside new graves. He said quietly, "My hands, ma'am. If you'd cut me free of this saddle horn . . ."

She looked at his face, but there was no way of knowing what she really saw. Slowly, she raised the Prescott and moved toward him until the muzzle was only inches from his chest. "Ma'am," he said urgently. But her mind was somewhere else. When she looked at him the face she saw belonged to someone else.

Probably it was Olive who saved his life unintentionally. As a legionnaire, Olive knew how hopeless it was to try to reason with *cafard*. He decided to take direct action now, while he still had a little of his strength left and the madwoman

108

had her attention on Cameron. Olive shot a glance, half grinning, at Cameron, and began gathering himself for a lunge.

Cameron did not have any decision to make, he had already decided that he would rather take his chances with a madwoman than with the legionnaire. He spoke quietly, almost in a conversational tone. "Behind you, ma'am."

She wheeled suddenly and fired. The bullet struck the ground to Olive's right and went screaming into the dazzling blue sky. The legionnaire froze.

"It's all right now," Cameron heard himself saying, in a tone that he might have used with a frightened colt.

After a moment of humming silence, she lowered the muzzle just a little. She looked sharply at Cameron and seemed to see him for the first time. Still, several long and uneasy seconds passed before she asked, "Who are you?"

"My name's Cameron, ma'am."

"You're a southern officer?"

"There are no more southern officers," he told her. "No more South—the way we used to know it."

"Who is he?" she asked, nodding toward Olive.

"The military government in Louisiana put a price on my head—he's taking me back."

"He's not a Southerner. Not even a Yankee, from the way he talks."

"He's English," Cameron said, hoping that she would be satisfied with that. He didn't think that she was in any condition to understand about Maximilian and the Foreign Legion. She understood about bounty hunters and that was enough.

"Why did you come here? What do you want?"

Cameron smiled wryly. "I didn't have any say about it. We were looking for water and something to eat."

She let this roll into her mind. There was a return of blankness in her expression. She continued to look up at Cameron. "You fought at The Wilderness?" she asked.

Cameron nodded.

"My husband was at The Wilderness. They buried him there."

". . . I'm sorry, ma'am," Cameron said quietly.

She looked at the heavy fighting knife in her hand and seemed surprised to see it there. She studied Cameron's face intently and appeared to be satisfied with what she saw. She placed the razor edge of the knife to the ropes and quickly cut him free.

Cameron rubbed his wrists, then climbed down.

Olive, whose face was slowly changing from leathery brown to dirty gray, glared at the man who had been his prisoner. Then he fell heavily on his face, and the dry earth slowly soaked up his blood.

Cameron went to him and turned him over.

The legionnaire's face was now as gray as death. "Olive, can you hear me?"

Olive stared at him with blank eyes.

"Is he dead?" the woman asked, only mildly interested.

"No, but he's losing a lot of blood."

She shrugged. "One more grave, more or less. It won't make any difference when they come."

Cameron shot her a quick look. "When who comes?"

She smiled in a way that left Cameron cold. "I don't know. His friends, I guess—if tax collectors have friends. The scalawag police over at Starr."

"You killed a tax collector?" Cameron asked.

The woman nodded. "His name was Dodd. Brought two slackers with him—call themselves policemen now." She looked out at the two mounds of raw red earth. "Jamie Hugh dug the graves and helped with the burying. Jamie's not very bright, even if he does wear a police badge. You wouldn't believe the way he carried on. He thought I was going to kill him too."

Cameron groaned to himself. Killing a tax collector was bad, and killing a military policeman was worse. But worst of all was having a witness, as he knew from grim experience. "Where is Jamie now?"

"Went back to Starr, I guess. That's four, five hours to the north."

"How long has Jamie been gone?"

She looked up at the sun and made a silent calculation. She seemed totally indifferent to what the future might hold for her. "About five hours."

Starr, Cameron guessed, must be the county seat, if the tax collector had been headquartered there. No doubt Jamie had told his story by this time, and a posse of policemen was sure to be headed for the scene of the crime.

Olive groaned. Cameron quickly inspected the area around the wound and decided that no bones had been broken. Olive ground his teeth but was silent while Cameron dragged him across the yard and laid him in the shade of the adobe hut. Methodically, almost without thinking, Cameron ripped the sleeve out of the legionnaire's shirt, folded it into two bandage pads, and bound them over the wound. Olive watched the operation in bewilderment and disbelief.

"You're going to let it go at this?" he asked incredulously.

"The government police will be here in a matter of a few hours. This bandage will hold you until then."

Cameron rose to his feet and Olive glared at him. It did not make sense, but the fact that Cameron was so matter-of-factly handling him, his life, outraged him. He lurched up on one elbow and laughed bitterly. "You Confederates are worse than the French! Honor—is that what

112

you're thinking? You know, don't you, that I'll be after you again if you don't kill me."

"Not soon," Cameron said dryly, "with that shoulder."

Great beads of sweat formed on Olive's face, and even the sweat had the stench of anger in it. "I'm telling you, Captain, I intend to collect that bounty!"

Maddeningly to the legionnaire, Cameron merely turned and walked away. Kate Barringer was standing in the doorway of the hut, staring out at the hills of brush and cactus. "He means it," she said, without actually looking at Cameron. "You ought to kill him now while you have the chance."

Cameron knew that honor among soldiers was out of fashion. He also knew that many brave Southerners would still be alive if their thinking had not been saturated with archaic codes and unrealistic convictions of what a gentleman could and could not do in the field. He realized that to kill Olive here, now, was only common sense—he had killed far better men for much less reason. Instead, he worried about what to do with the woman.

She told him, "There's not much food here but . . ." She smiled. It was a taut, glittering smile, but perfectly sane and a little sad. "I won't be needing it for myself much longer. You might as well help yourself."

She showed Cameron to a small mound of corn pones that had been cooked in a skillet at a corner fireplace. And she showed him a pot of stew with meat that tasted like rabbit and wild onions and other plant roots that Cameron could not identify. He could not say that it was good, but he wolfed it greedily. "Can you ride?" he asked at last, putting aside the empty pot.

"When I was a young girl . . . But I haven't seen a sidesaddle since we moved to Texas."

"A sidesaddle wouldn't be any good anyway. Get a few things together, only necessary things, and I'll make a blanket roll."

She shook her head slowly. "No, I can't leave this place. Karl worked too hard to get a start here. I can't leave it now."

"Don't you realize what will happen to you," Cameron said impatiently, "if Jamie brings a posse of government police back with him—as he's bound to do?"

She had thought about it, but not all the way to the end. She thought about it now. "They'll hang me?" she asked at last.

"Or worse. These aren't soldiers you're dealing with, they're southern trash who've turned against their own."

She nodded. "That's right enough." She looked aimlessly about the hut. Weariness and despair were etched in her face, and in a way it was worse than the madness had been. "Karl worked so hard on this place," she said to no one in particular. "Before the war he said that one day all these wild cattle here in the brush country would make us rich. Of course there wasn't much market for cattle then. A few head got shipped to New Orleans, but most of what he caught he sold to hide and tallow contractors. But one day, he said, when the soldiers and the rangers got the Comanches tamed, there would be big roads opened to the North. People up there were hungry for beef, he said. And Lord knows we've got plenty of it down here, if you can catch it in all this brush . . ."

"Ma'am," Cameron said impatiently, "if you'd just get a few things together."

She didn't appear to hear him. "Do you think it'll ever happen?" she asked him. "Those big cattle roads, I mean, that Karl believed in?"

Cameron had to admit that he knew very little about the cattle business, but that such roads sounded reasonable enough, once the Comanches and other Plains tribes were contained on reservations.

She shrugged. "Well, it doesn't matter now. I had two Mex *vaqueros*, good hands. They caught the cows and we sold enough to scrape by. Until that new tax collector came. Him and his slacker policemen scared off my *vaqueros*. They shot the cows they gathered and skinned them—the new government at the county seat had to have

115

its taxes, one way or another, they said. And they pulled down the brush corral—the one that Karl had built before riding off to war with General Hood. I don't know. . . ." She looked intently at Cameron. "When they pulled down the corral and shot the cattle—somehow it was like they had killed Karl all over again. That was when I killed them, and why I killed them, in case you're wondering."

Cameron was acutely aware of the passage of time. "Pretty soon the government in Washington will send other men down here—honest judges and administrators—and then people like us can expect a fair trial. But not now."

She seemed to agree with everything he said, but she shook her head. "I know . . . but I can't go."

"You can't stay," he told her. "They won't let you."

She stared out at the wild country that had once seemed to hold so much promise for her husband. Then she moved listlessly about the hut. Cameron paced back and forth in the gravelly doorway; the passing of minutes put his nerves on edge.

Gray-faced, Olive watched him with a bitter sneer. "You're even a bigger fool than I thought, Captain, if you drag that crazy woman with you. It'll just make it twice as easy for me to find you."

Cameron glanced at him curiously. "Are you afraid of not earning your bounty?"

Olive's mouth twisted. He seemed to be laughing silently. "I don't worry about earning it, just so I get it—and I will. But I wonder where you think you can run to. Back to Mexico? You'd have the whole Juárez army to deal with. And if you didn't run into that, there'd be the Indians. And if not the Indians, then the Mexicans, who think you killed the priest in Monterrey. Or the French, who'll think you helped a legionnaire desert."

Olive paused. "That takes care of Mexico. And you're not much better off in Texas, with renegade Southerners and northern scavengers running the country. A thousand-dollar bounty on your head. Wanted for murder."

Cameron stared at him fixedly, as he might have stared at a five-legged calf. He had seen examples of the legionnaire's cold-bloodedness and efficiency, and he knew that Olive was not mouthing empty threats.

Olive's face was slack and colorless, but his eyes glittered. "You thinking about killing me, Captain?" he taunted. "Murder . . . we think about it, all of us, at one time or other. Killing me wouldn't solve all your problems, but it would make most of them a lot easier to live with. But you won't do it. Behaviour unbecoming to an officer and a gentleman!" He started to laugh, but

117

the sound ended in a gasp of pain. When he got his breath he went on, his voice dripping hate. "The trouble with you, Captain, is you're a fool. And there's one thing a fool can never do. He can never change the thing he is."

Cameron felt his face warming. It was true that, in the back of his mind, he had quietly considered murder. But he could not do it. It was as simple as that. He said stiffly, "That bounty money means a lot to you, doesn't it?"

Olive stared at him. "To a man who's served the Legion; almost seven years at two francs a month?" He could not begin to explain to this former gentleman of leisure how immense a fortune of a thousand dollars could be.

Cameron said, "I have friends of means—or used to have. It's just possible that I could get the money for you."

Olive smiled knowingly. He was a man who could appreciate a good rear-guard action. "Forget it, Captain. It's more than the money I want. It's the reputation. The reputation that Trent had wanted to make for himself. There'll be others after you, maybe with even bigger prices on their heads. A man," he added dryly, "has got to look to his future."

Kate Barringer sat on a three-legged stool in the center of the small room and saw a hundred things that she had scarcely noticed before. The crumbly, sun-cured adobe blocks, the pounded clay floor, the grayish gypsum-plastered interior. Everywhere she looked there was something to remind her of Karl.

Karl had been a small man physically, but his thinking had been scaled for giants. He had had boundless faith in his future cattle roads to the North. He had even talked to other wild cow hunters with the idea of getting together a great herd and driving it the length of Texas, then up the Shawnee Trace through Indian Territory, to Missouri. The other cow hunters had called him loco. Then came the war, and Karl's imagination had been captured by the call of a different trumpet.

"Ma'am," Cameron said quietly from the doorway, "we can't wait any longer."

She turned and looked at him. "I've been thinking about my husband," she said wonderingly. "About all the things he did and wanted to do. And do you know something? I can't remember what he looked like."

"Four years of war, ma'am. It's a long time."

"Oh, I recollect in a general way. He was not much taller than I am, and he was gentle, and he almost never raised his voice, even to a balky team. I used to be able to close my eyes and see his face, like he was right in front of me—I can't do it now. I can't see anything at all."

Cameron stood silent for several seconds.

At last she stood up and quietly folded a shirt-waist and a black skirt. With these and a few other items of clothing she made a parcel about the size of a large cigar can.

"Is that all?" Cameron asked.

"Yes."

"Where are the guns? The deputies . . ." The ones in their graves. "The deputies must have had rifles or pistols."

"I don't know." She looked blank. "Maybe Jamie took them to Starr with him."

Something else occurred to Cameron. "When we rode up you had just the musket. How did you manage to kill two men with a single-shot weapon?"

She appeared to give the question long and sober thought. At last she said, "I think I shot Pete Rolly with his own pistol."

That reply should have told Cameron something, but it didn't. The matter of missing weapons still disturbed his military mind. Maybe Jamie wasn't very smart, but apparently he was smart enough to have gathered up the guns before pulling out.

"Well . . ." Cameron said resignedly. Kate Barringer looked at him, then she turned and looked at the hut for the last time.

They left the hut and walked to the horses.

SIX

Colonel Montfort's black gelding began to limp toward midafternoon, and by the time Cameron located the piece of flint in the frog, it was too late. The animal was lame. Cameron stripped the black and let it go. Then he hid the rig in a dry wash and covered it with brush.

Cameron felt that the incident was a bad omen, but to Kate Barringer he smiled with strained cheerfulness. "Well, we didn't need a pack animal anyway. We can travel faster without one." They drank sparingly from Roger Trent's canteen, which they had filled at the Barringer well. "Are you tired?" he asked.

"No." They had been riding almost four hours and this was the first word she had spoken. Like a plainsman, she glanced up at the sun and then down at her own shadow and judged the time. "Jamie's had plenty time to make it to Starr and back." She smiled wanly. "Unless his horse stepped in a doghole along the way. Most likely the state police, as they call themselves, are at the 'dobe, or looking into the graves."

Or scouting the brush country for a tree big enough to support a hanging rope, Cameron thought. "Do you know a place called Bellah's Post Office?" he asked.

"I know something about it. There's a rendering and tanning plant. The hide and tallow commission men headquarters are there; Karl used to sell them part of his gather."

She answered quickly enough, and Cameron could not discover any trace of hysteria in anything she said or did, but in her eyes there was a profound dullness that worried him. "Do you think you could find the place?"

She appeared to consider the question, but he could see that her mind was on other things. "I think so," she said after a long pause. "It's on a river, Rio Blanco—I remember Karl mentioning it. This time of year it's usually dry." She made an effort at concentration. "We must be close to it now. About two hours east of Starr, Karl said. The town is north a way from there."

Since leaving the adobe, Cameron had been threshing his memory in an effort to think of a Texan whom he knew and could trust. The name that finally came to him was Archer. Captain Paul Brooks Archer, a troop commander in the First Texas Cavalry. Cameron hadn't seen him since the Pennsylvania campaign, but now he remembered that Archer had lived in a small South Texas town—Bellah's Post Office.

Now as they rode north, Cameron searched the crowded corners of his mind for bits of trickery that he had learned from old line officers of the Indian fighting cavalry. He employed brush drags to confuse the trail. They rode on shale and rock whenever possible, and along the windward lips of gullies and arroyos. Sometimes, between key points, they even rode backwards. None of it appeared to interest Kate Barringer in the least.

When they found the Rio Blanco its bed was dazzling white sand. They continued north along the rocky bank.

With a subtle shift of wind Kate Barringer shook free of the dark thoughts that had seized her. She looked sharply at Cameron, and he said, "The tanning vats at Bellah's Post Office. And the rendering plant." But for a moment Cameron was in the war again, approaching the field of yesterday's battle, where the blood-soaked ground was littered with bloated corpses of horses and men and a sickening stench rose in shimmering waves and made the air heavy with rottenness.

The town was about what Cameron expected. A handful of mud huts scattered without plan along the bank of the dry river, a string of loosely connected shacks that housed the cookers and the tanning vats. Cameron reined to a halt and motioned Kate Barringer to do the same. "I'd better go the rest of the way alone," he told her. "I'm not sure what I'll find here, and it's just as well that we're not seen together."

They backtracked for a short distance and Cameron led the roan down the clay bank and staked it. Kate Barringer accepted it all without question. "You'll be all right here," he told her. "I won't be any longer than I have to."

She looked at him with a wry hint of a smile. She didn't believe him. There was no doubt in her mind that he had decided to rid himself of a needless burden and that she would never see him again. Cameron unsheathed the Henry that he had picked up by the well. "Here, you'd better keep this until I get back."

She accepted the rifle with indifference. Cameron looked at her and for the first time saw her and thought of her as a person. She was not very old—no more than twenty-three or -four. This realization surprised him. Somehow, without actually giving it any thought, he had assumed that she was much older. She must have been rather pretty at one time, and perhaps she still would be if it hadn't been for the hair stringing in her eyes, her dirt-smeared face and almost idiot-like blankness of expression.

Then Cameron rubbed his hand over his own face, feeling the stubble of beard and the dirt, and he realized that he was not quite the cavalier that he had once been several lifetimes ago, before the war.

Bellah's Post Office, like so many other towns and cities of the South, was a casualty of the war.

Once it had been a market town for cow hunters, and then a way station on the Carrizo-Laredo stage line, finally achieving the official status of "post office." Now it was none of those things. Like so many other post-war towns, it stank of despair.

In a rawhide corral near the tannery there was a small bunch of wild horses, animals that mustangers had caught and sold for hide and tallow—one of the many unpleasant jobs that men of the South had resorted to in order to stay alive. The small horses huffed and stamped, wild-eyed with fear as they waited to be reduced to shoe-leather and a few pounds of fat. In another corral were wild cattle. They too stirred nervously at the approach of the rider, and in the tightly packed enclosure the clashing of their great curved horns resounded like pistol shots.

Behind the cooking shacks was a mountain of gleaming white bones, and in the dry river bed another mountain, the rotting parts of carcasses that the hide and tallow men had found no profitable use for. Around this mountain hovered blowflies by the millions, and the river bed was black with carrion birds, pecking, tearing, gobbling and occasionally shrieking angrily as some huge turkey buzzard waded sluggishly through their seething numbers.

Cameron had seen worse things in his time—

nevertheless, he had to keep a tight rein on his rising stomach.

An old woman came out of one of the shacks, dashed some dirty water on the ground, and stared idly as Cameron rode toward the cooking shacks. To be stared at was not surprising; it was not likely that Bellah's Post Office got many visitors.

A man came out of one of the tanning huts and stood gazing at Cameron with dull interest as he filled and lighted a cob pipe. Cameron reined toward him.

"I'm looking for an old friend. Captain Archer. Paul Brooks Archer."

The man, as black as a fieldworker, grinned unpleasantly. "Cap'n Paul Brooks Archer," he said mockingly. "Now what'd you be wantin' with Cap'n Archer?"

"It's a matter of . . . it's personal." A strange discomfort took hold of Cameron.

The man's grin was almost a sneer. Everything about him struck unpleasant chords. At the same time he was arrogant and cringing. Mocking and angry. Despairing and rebellious. He moved forward slowly and Cameron saw for the first time that his left trouser leg flapped loosely about a wooden stump. His clothing, now the color of greasy slate, had once been a Confederate officer's uniform. He gazed up at Cameron and, without actually moving, seemed to shrug.

"All right, Captain." It sounded like a sigh. "What is it you want from your old friend, Paul Archer?"

Cameron stared. Could this be the brash, friendly young officer that he had known at the beginning of the war?

The man laughed. It sounded like blasphemy. "That's right, Captain Cameron, your old friend Paul Archer is now an apprentice hide tanner, and lucky to have the job." He rapped his wooden stump with his fist. "You might be amazed to know how little demand there is nowadays for one-legged cavalry officers." He scowled, and the skin of his face and hands looked as thick and wrinkled as buffalo hide. With a little more warmth, but just a little, he said, "What is it that brings you to Texas?"

Receiving no invitation to dismount, Cameron remained in the saddle. "For one reason, I can't go back to Louisiana." His bones were sagging badly. What kind of help could he expect from a man who was not even in a position to help himself?

"Trouble?" Archer asked, as though making idle conversation. "With the new military government?"

"It's not a military government, strictly speaking. The new officials are turncoats and scalawags, the Yankees keep their soldiers out of it as much as possible."

"Who was it you killed?" Archer asked, as if it was the most natural of questions.

Cameron hesitated. "A tax collector, as they now call themselves. Man by the name of Jeffers, who the Yankees made the mayor. He and his turncoat friends were driving off my livestock. When I tried to stop them, they attacked me. No free court would convict me—but that's something we don't have in Louisiana right now."

Archer laughed again, that same harsh sound that grated on Cameron's nerves. "They must of put a pretty price on your scalp for a thing like that."

Cameron shifted uneasily. "I need help, Archer, even if it's only information. I know I can't go back to Louisiana. And striking north would be out of the question . . ."

"Lot of old soldiers striking for Mexico," Archer interrupted.

Cameron shook his head. "Mexico's out for me. The only direction I've got is west. And all I know about the country west of here is what I remember from the times you used to talk about it."

Archer's eyes turned curiously blank. Perhaps he was recalling the hundreds of campfires that he had huddled close to, as so many other soldiers had done, miserable and homesick and frightened. And the yarns they told about their homelands. To a soldier wet to the skin on a winter night, even a place like Bellah's Post Office could seem like a small corner of paradise.

His eyes came back in focus. "Your best chance," he said, "is to strike east. Make for one of the Gulf ports and catch a ship. South America, maybe. Until things get better."

Cameron had already thought of those Gulf ports, but Union officials were sure to be thick in such places. Besides, there was the woman, Kate Barringer, to think about. She was now as much a fugitive as he was. "It wouldn't work," he said, thinking aloud. "Not with a woman to look out for."

"A woman?" Archer's indifference had suddenly vanished. His eyes, eerily pale in his dark face, stared up at Cameron. "Her name wouldn't be Kate Barringer, would it?"

Cameron's obvious anger at himself was all the answer that Archer needed. "By yourself you'd have a chance catchin' a boat at Corpus. But you won't have a chance there, or anywhere else, as long as you've got that woman with you."

"How," Cameron asked coldly, "did you know about Kate Barringer?"

"One of those new sheriff's deputies was this way not long before you rode in. The sheriff, soon's he heard about the killin', sent deputies ridin' in all directions."

Cameron sat rigid in the saddle. Things were moving much faster than he had counted on. Like

Kate Barringer, he had believed that the lawmen would first make for the scene of the shooting to verify Jamie's story.

"Sorry, Cameron," Archer said, eager to disassociate himself from the whole affair. "I can't help you. A man with one leg shot away has got enough trouble just tryin' to stay alive. Strike any way you please, but take my advice and get rid of the woman."

Cameron made himself swallow his anger. "We don't have any food, Archer, and Lord knows where we'll find any. If you could let us have some dried beef or . . ."

Archer cut in quickly. "I already told you. There's nothin' I can do." He turned awkwardly and hobbled back toward the tanning shed. ". . . Except," he added, after he had stopped for a moment and thought it over, "except . . . there might be a place where you could hole up for a day or two. Where the bluebelly police won't find you."

Cameron felt as if he had broken out of murky darkness into the light. "I'd be much obliged for anything at all. . . ."

Impatiently, Archer waved away all thanks. "Head north of here for maybe an hour. Then bear west, back toward the Bravo, until you come to an arroyo grown over with salt cedars. A little water gets through in early spring, but the cedars keep it sapped dry the rest of the year. Head north again along the wash, and after a while you'll come to a limestone shelf. Back of the shelf there's a cave." His taut smile was devoid of humor. "Favorite hideout for Mex *bandidos* not so long ago. Before they all joined up with Juárez."

Cameron rubbed his chin uncertainly. "Won't the police know about the cave?"

Archer's abrupt laughter was as humorless as his smile. "All the new police know about is taxes, and foreclosures, and more taxes." He seemed to retreat behind a grim wall of thought. "Just a minute," he said, "before you go."

Archer hobbled across the road and entered one of the flimsy shacks. In a few minutes he returned and handed Cameron a small parcel. It was wrapped in a greasy and ancient newspaper; its headlines still had the South winning the war. "It's not much. Corn dogs and fried beef, but it'll hold your ribs apart for a day or so."

Cameron nodded his gratitude. "Maybe I'll be able to repay you someday."

"The way you can repay me is to ride out of here before somebody guesses who you are. And don't mention my name if you get yourself caught."

Cameron reined his dun into the dry wash. Kate Barringer was sitting with her back against the clay wall in an attitude of dull exhaustion. "The

131

foray wasn't all it might have been," he said with forced cheerfulness, "but it wasn't a complete failure either." He showed her the parcel. "Something to hold off hunger for a little while. And a place where we can rest up tonight. Until we get an idea what the police are up to."

She wasn't especially impressed. But then, neither was Cameron. He had hoped for a change of clothing so that he wouldn't be quite so conspicuously a former Confederate officer. And the loan of a wagon and team which, for the moment, would be much safer than horsebacking. A young farm wife on a wagon seat would not arouse much suspicion—a young woman riding a stock saddle in an ordinary house dress was something else altogether.

"We'd better get started," he said. "If you feel up to a little more riding."

She nodded dully. "Yes. I'm all right."

She didn't ask where they were going, and Cameron decided that it was just as well. When they rode out of the wash all the old war-learned senses seemed to rise to the surface of Cameron's skin. He was seized by a sensation of nakedness, of moving across an invisible threshold into a zone of acute danger. The sensation was so intense that he shot a glance at Kate Barringer to see if she had felt it.

But her expression of dullness had not changed. It was the war, he decided. Too many hours of anxious waiting, the blood cold and still in his veins, for the trumpeter to sound the *charge*. He had lived too long with the expectation of sudden death.

William Olive, a credit to the methods of training and conditioning of the *Légion Etrangère*, waited stoically for whatever was to come.

At the moment there was nothing he could do to change his predicament, so he did not waste his energy in thinking about it. He could feel the musket ball, like a white-hot ingot imbedded in his flesh—that would have to come out. Until it did, moving about would only hurry the process of infection.

So he made himself as comfortable as possible, lying in the weed-grown yard of Kate Barringer's hut, and thought of many things. For a long while he thought, with great pleasure, about Sergent-Chef Giuseppe Ciano. The *late* Sergent-Chef Giuseppe Ciano. But there was a limit to how long he could rejoice in something as commonplace as death.

His thoughts moved to other things. Giving due consideration to his present troubles, Olive was not too displeased with the way his luck had run. After all, what was a shoulder wound compared to freedom from the Legion? More important, there was the wealth that would be his when he collected the bounty.

He took it as ironic justice that the woman who had shot him might well be responsible for his recapturing Cameron. It was conceivable that Cameron alone might cover his trail well enough to lose even a manhunter of Olive's talent and experience. But Cameron burdened with a woman, never.

Olive didn't remember losing consciousness, just the rough hand shaking his unhurt shoulder. "Come alive, mister! Jamie, come here! You ever see this bird before?"

Olive opened his eyes and was dimly surprised to see that it was almost dark. He felt heavy and sluggish, and there was a brightly burning fire in his left shoulder. Blurred figures moved back and forth across the dooryard. For one disturbing moment Olive was unable to recall what had happened, or where he was, or what he was doing here.

A drawling, lazy-sounding voice was saying, "Paper here says Trent. Roger Trent. Some kind of detective, looks like."

"Jamie!" the first man yelled. "Get yourself over here!"

Olive's vision cleared slowly. He began to piece things together in his mind and make a reasonable guess as to what was happening. These men must be the new government policemen come to investigate the killings.

The hand was again shaking Olive's shoulder,

and he felt his wound beginning to bleed again. The senselessness of the act enraged the legionnaire more than a direct attack would have done. He said coldly, as soon as he was capable of speaking, "Take your bloody hands off me before I rip you open crotch to gullet."

The shaker looked as startled as if a corpse had come alive in his hands. A portly, soft, pink-cheeked man, he stepped quickly back and eyed Olive cautiously. "Your name Trent?" he asked.

They had gone through his pockets and found the papers that he had taken from the detective. Well, that was all right. Let them think he was a detective if they wanted to. He said thickly, "What if I am? Who are you?"

"County Sheriff," the pink-cheeked man said pompously. "Arvin Waller. We're investigatin' these here murders of my deputies. You're in a pretty fix, you know. Exactly what was your part in the killin's? You might as well tell us now— we'll get the straight of it sooner or later."

Olive could have laughed. He had seen Waller's kind many times. The Wallers of the earth always played it safe. They were the fence straddlers who never took sides until they were sure who the winner was going to be. They were known as turncoats and scalawags and a hundred other names that were unprintable, and they were despised by all. Still, in that hectic tragic period between the time a nation is defeated and the time it is taken over by responsible officials, the Arvin Wallers were quick to fill the vacuum.

The hulking, vaguely bewildered-looking youth had shambled up beside the sheriff. He was slowly shaking his head from side to side.

"I never seen this feller before, Sheriff."

"He wasn't here when Pete and Mr. Dodd was killed?"

Still shaking his heavy head, Jamie said, "Wasn't nobody here but just me and Pete Rolly and the tax collector. And Missus Barringer that done the shootin'."

"Then what's *he* doin' here?" the sheriff demanded, pointing at Olive.

Jamie shrugged. He had said all he had to say on the subject, so he shambled back toward the corral where some men were digging up one of the bodies. The sheriff, instinctively distrustful of all men, glared at the man beside him. "Webb, what else did you find in his pockets?"

Webb who, like all the others, wore a deputy's badge, showed Waller the papers. "Just these wanted posters. And some arrest warrants," he answered sharply at his boss. "Here's somethin'. U.S. marshal's commission, signed by a judge in Louisiana."

This bit of intelligence worked miracles on the sheriff's face. Faster than Olive could follow the changes, his expression went from surprise to wonderment, to dismay, to a kind of fawning servility. "U.S. marshal!" he said worriedly. "Why didn't you say so?"

"You didn't ask." Olive's tone was accusing. "But now that you know maybe you'd better pay some attention to my wound."

The sheriff shifted from one foot to the other. From his hip pocket he produced a blue bandanna and mopped his pink face. "The closest doc in these parts is at Starr. Webb, see if you can rustle up a hack of some kind for the marshal."

"No hacks around here," Webb replied.

The diggers had recovered one body and were working on the second grave. "Who was it shot you?" the sheriff asked at last.

"Man I was trailing . . . Wanted by the Louisiana authorities. He wouldn't mean anything to you."

Waller quickly agreed that Louisiana's troubles could not be any affair of his. Sometimes these new lords of the South came in strange packages. Best to handle them gently, and with gloves on, the way you'd do with a copperhead. "Well," the sheriff said, "it's all the same to me. Long's it's got nothin' to do with the woman, of course. Kate Barringer."

With something akin to pity—pity for the South in general and Texas in particular—Olive looked at this present example of law-enforcement officer. But he said nothing. Kate Barringer, if that was her name, was the star that would eventually lead him to Cameron, and he didn't intend to let these bunglers add their irritating brand of confusion to the problem.

Cameron had no trouble finding the arroyo. Following Archer's directions, he discovered the shelf of limestone, just as Archer had promised, and back of the shelf, amid a writhing tangle of cedar roots, the *bandido* cave.

It was not actually a cave but merely an erosion in the bank of the wash, caused by countless years of spring rains and flash floods and cedar roots that were tougher than stone. The roof, formed by the great slab of limestone, was blackened by old outlaw fires.

It looked like a safe place. An almost impossible place to get to, unless you had precise directions. The heavy growth of salt cedar stood solid guard on either bank. A regiment of cavalry could have moved down that deep gully and, from a quarter-mile away, never be seen or heard.

"No clean sheets," Cameron said with an easy smile, "but it looks snug enough for now. Tomorrow I'll do some scouting. Somewhere, even in this country, there must be some old soldiers who'd be willing to help a fellow officer."

Kate Barringer looked at him from the corner of her eyes, the way she might have looked at a man gone slightly mad.

Suddenly Cameron thought of something. "Mrs. Barringer, is there a Freemason lodge in Starr?"

She shot him another of her suspicious looks. "If there is, I never heard about it."

"Do you know of anyone who belongs to the lodge?"

She shook her head slowly. "Why?"

It wasn't easy to explain. Freemasonry meant different things to different men. To some it was a lark. To others it was a kind of duty that one fell heir to in the normal course of things, like joining a church. To a few, Freemasonry itself was almost a religion. It was fancy uniforms and silver swords and secret passwords and handshakes. It was . . . *Freemasonry*.

And it was power, as armies and nations had learned in the years since 1861. More than one northern potentate had received favors and even military information from southern initiates. The number of southern Masonic officers who had "escaped" from northern prison camps, sometimes escorted royally by lower-ranking northern lodge brothers, was too embarrassing for the Union authorities to keep record of.

These things Cameron sketchily explained. Kate Barringer listened with growing wonder. "I hadn't realized men were such fools."

Cameron laughed. "It's not all foolishness. For you and me it could be the difference between hanging or going free. If I could just find a Mason. The right kind of Mason."

"Are you one?"

"Before the war I was." He frowned in thought. "Who's the most important man in Starr?"

"Now, or before the scalawags?"

"Before."

He could see her thoughts moving cautiously into the past, carefully avoiding all that was personal or painful. "Otis Blackman," she said at last. "He owns the biggest store. Sometimes he lends money. He got a mail route through the county singlehanded. And over to the east somewhere there're Blackman cotton fields." She shot him a narrow look. "They *do* say that Blackman cotton had better luck than most in running the blockade."

Cameron smiled thinly. "I don't like the notion of making a trip to Starr, but it might be worth the risk if I can talk to Blackman."

For a while they were almost comfortable in that dark, cool recess beneath the great rock slab. They had no coffee so there was no need to make a fire. They divided the greasy corn dogs and the fried beef and ate in long, thoughtful silence. The late sun glowed like a bed of live coals through the lacework of salt cedar. Cameron let his mind work on Blackman.

Busy with his own thoughts, he almost forgot about the woman. But now he looked at her.

For a moment her eyes were as vacant as the windows of a burned-out house. Her hands, one of them still squeezing the greasy crumbs of a corn dog, were clenched and white-knuckled on her lap. Her face had that curious appearance of stone that Cameron had seen in the faces of soldiers after a particularly long and bloody battle.

"Mrs. Barringer . . . ?" Cameron's concern showed in his voice. She turned her head and looked at him with that chilling vacancy.

"Mrs. Barringer!" This time there was more than concern in his voice.

Slowly, the stone face began to soften. ". . . I'm sorry," she said at last.

"What about?" Cameron knew from experience that the best medicine in some cases was talk. "Is it losing your place? The adobe, the sheds, the corrals? All the things that your husband worked to build?"

"No." She shook her head. "I wasn't thinking about that."

Cameron knew what ailed her. It was a certain sickness of the soul that came, sooner or later, to almost every soldier. It was a sickness for which there was no cure. It had to be lived with.

"The two men?" he asked with deliberate matter-of-factness. "The ones you had to kill?"

She nodded.

"Killing is never a simple thing," he told her.

"Some soldiers never learn to live with it. They go mad."

She looked at him strangely. "Do you think I'm going mad?"

"No. You showed grit in standing up to them."

She was still looking at him in that strange way. "You don't know why I did it, do you?"

"Yes, ma'am, you told me. They were stealing your stock and tearing down the corral."

"Is that what I said?" She shook her head, as if puzzled. "I don't know if I can explain it. But I've got to try."

Cameron very carefully said nothing.

"When they first rode up to the 'dobe I saw that Pete Rolly was drunk. Early in the war, when all the men were volunteering to fight the war, Pete joined the Rangers to hold off the Comanches. But when he was up in the Panhandle he deserted the Rangers and joined a bunch of Comancheros. He spent the war selling whisky and guns to the Indians." She shrugged wearily and, finger by finger, began to unclench her fists. "Pete's the kind we've got now. They call themselves police."

"They won't last."

"But they're what we've got." For a full minute or longer she was silent. Then she said, "They were laughing. Pete and the new tax collector called Dodd. I watched them tearing down the brush fence, destroying the corral that Karl had built. I don't know . . . it was like watching them kill Karl all over again. Watching them destroy the things he had built. And running off the cattle. I tried to make them stop. But they went on laughing and wrecking things. I ran back to the 'dobe and got that old musket down from the wall and loaded it."

She stared at the smear of grease and cornmeal on her hand. "I guess they thought it was a joke," she said. " 'Don't you go and hurt yourself with that contraption,' Pete Rolly told me. 'Smart-looking women are kind of scarce in these parts. I wouldn't want you to go and get yourself hurt.' Then he laughed some more. But the tax collector, Dodd, was beginning to see that it was no joke. He ordered me to put the musket down. When I didn't do it, he tried to take it away from me. And that was when I shot him."

She looked at Cameron. "It was a fool thing for him to do. I didn't want to shoot him. I only wanted them to stop killing Karl. I remember hearing the musket go off and feeling the kick, and then the tax collector was on the ground, kicking and moaning, and in a matter of minutes he was dead. Pete didn't quite believe it. His face was white as a sheet. He kept shaking Dodd and telling him to snap out of it. But Dodd was dead. And finally even Pete Rolly came to believe it. He looked at me for a long time and kind of rubbed his hand across his mouth, like a man that had just pulled up to well-set table. When Jamie heard the shot he started running toward the 'dobe, but Pete hollered for him to catch the cattle that were pouring out of the broken corral. Jamie wasn't one to argue. He did what Pete told him."

Cameron handed her his faded bandanna and she wiped the crushed corn dog from her hands. At last she went on. "Pete knew that I couldn't use the musket again without reloading, so he wasn't afraid. He looked at me and then at the dead tax collector. And then he said, 'Well, Dodd never amounted to much, anyhow. Of course, back in Starr there'll be a big ruckus. Missy, that's when you're goin' to need a friend. And old Pete Rolly can be a real good friend, if he's treated right.' I didn't know yet what he was getting at. But I could see the drunken glitter in his eyes. He went on talking, and as he talked he started toward me. And it was then that I began to suspect . . ."

And Cameron was just beginning to understand the ugliness that had prompted Kate Barringer's toneless recital. He wanted to tell her that he understood and that she needn't go on. But he didn't do it. Medicine half swallowed could not help her. She had to talk it out.

She made a senseless gesture with one hand.

"Somehow I had the notion that poor, slow-witted Jamie could help me. When I understood the look in Pete's eyes I began to shout for Jamie. Pete hit me across the face, grinning as he did it. And my shout for help never got past my lips. And anyway, Jamie was lost in the brush by that time, hopelessly looking for the lost stock. I turned and ran for the 'dobe. But Pete was at the door long before I could reload the musket. He kicked the latch off the door. Then he just stood there in the doorway, staring at me. 'Missy,' he told me, 'like I said, you're goin' to need a friend when folks find out about the tax collector. But it don't really make any difference whether you're friendly or not. It'll all be the same in the long run. Crazy Jamie sure won't help you. And who back in Starr will take the word of a brush popper's woman over the word of a state policeman?' Then he laughed and came toward me."

She was back in that cramped adobe hut, and the drunk with the ugly eyes was coming toward her. "This," she said in a puzzled tone, "is the part I can't explain. I wasn't afraid of Pete Rolly—it wasn't that. It was just that I had watched him wrecking bits and pieces of my life and Karl's. And laughing as he did it. And now he had it in his mind to ruin the last thing in the world that had been my husband's—myself." She smiled at Cameron in a chilling way. "He forced me back against the cook table beside the fireplace. He touched me. I flinched and that made him angry.

145

He grabbed me with both hands, I stumbled and almost fell. That was when I grabbed his pistol . . ."

She shot an animal-quick look at Cameron. "I killed him. I don't actually remember doing it, but I killed him. The tax collector—that had been an accident. Not this. I looked down and there was Pete Rolly rolling on the floor, holding his chest. His hands were bloody and there were great fat tears cutting wet furrows down his dirty face. I threw the pistol into the yard, and then I sat down to wait for Jamie to come back."

That was all. She had put it into words, and now the nightmare was reality and could be dealt with as such. Cameron watched her, then got up and walked out of the cave. There was nothing he could do for her now except leave her alone.

He moved up the dry wash to where he had staked the horses. He emptied one of the canteens into his hat and divided the water evenly between the horses. As a cavalryman, he did not like the dull-eyed looks the animals gave him. They needed more water, a good rest, and several measures of grain in their bellies.

He moved on up the wash in the dim hopes of finding a patch of bunch grass in that bed of sterile sand. What he found was not grass but an abrupt outcrop of limestone jutting out of the bottom of the arroyo and, around the outcrop, a wild tangle of salt cedar.

Cameron stared at this sheer wall of stone and brush. He went up to it and inspected it closer.

Suddenly, it seemed, the westering sun had lost its warmth. Cameron felt a cold, familiar breath on the back of his neck. The arroyo was boxed. And had been so for a long time.

He thought about that, and he didn't like it. If Archer had known about the cave, he must also have known about this dead end. This quietly seductive trap, with a welcoming entrance but no exit. Cameron did not wonder that the Mexican *bandidos* no longer used it.

SEVEN

Kate Barringer's face was no longer an expressionless mask. Her eyes were reddish and puffy, and the sagging lines of exhaustion added years to her appearance. Still, Cameron much preferred the way she looked now to the way he had first found her.

She had met him at the mouth of the cave and immediately recognized the lines of worry in his own face. "Something's wrong?"

"I can't be sure. But I'm afraid that wartime friendships may not be as strong or permanent as I had hoped." She looked puzzled and he added, "This cave, the arroyo, even the salt cedars up there—they all add up to an almost perfect trap. The upstream end has been blocked, and has been for a long time. There's no way out of here except the way we came in . . . and I think we'd better be taking it as soon as we can."

She was quietly alert, a different person from the one he had left a short time before. "Your friend back at Bellah's Post Office?"

Cameron smiled grimly. "Captain Paul Brooks Archer. I'm afraid so." Not that Archer's treachery, if that was what it was, caused him any special bitterness. War had made life cheap, and treachery was commonplace. But thousand-dollar bounties came a man's way only once in a lifetime, if he was lucky. "I don't like to ask, but if you could ride on a little farther . . ."

"I'm all right, Captain." She colored slightly, remembering the ugliness that she had exposed to him.

It was almost dark by the time they reached the end of the cedar-roofed arroyo. There was no sign of Archer or the military police, but all the same Cameron breathed easier when they reached open prairie. "Which way is the county seat?"

She pointed. "It's full of police and sheriff's deputies, so they say."

"Just the same," Cameron thought aloud, "I'd like to see this man, Blackman, who had such good luck running the northern blockades."

"Do you think he will help us?"

"I don't know." Cameron smiled faintly. "Maybe. *If* he's a Mason. If he's a *good* Mason. If he happens to have powerful friends. And if he isn't too greedy."

Suddenly she smiled. It was more an expression of the eyes than of the mouth, and magically the years seemed to fall away from her. It was a fleeting thing, but for just a moment Cameron glimpsed the young woman that Karl Barringer had brought with him to Texas years ago. And he judged Karl Barringer to have been a lucky man.

They rode steadily for the best part of two

hours, skirting the small dense forests of brush, but keeping to the shadows whenever possible. Only occasionally did Cameron mount a crest to study their back trail.

The night was still, with only a breath of a breeze whispering up from the Bravo. Cameron was beginning to feel foolish. Had he thrown away a chance of real help from Archer?

What Kate Barringer thought, she did not put into words. She rode quietly and uncomplainingly. A pale moon faded behind a curtain of flying clouds, and the night was black.

The light, when it appeared, was startling in its contrast. Cameron reined up sharply, muttering under his breath. The light, reddish in color, mounted quickly into the desert sky and then seemed to settle and spread.

Kate Barringer looked at Cameron. "What is it?"

"I don't know." The color was much too red for sunrise, even if the time and direction had been right. "Wait here." He urged the weary dun to a mesquite-covered ridge and studied the garish light for several minutes.

He had never seen anything exactly like it before, but he knew what it was. Above the spreading light there was a certain billowing darkness that was unmistakable. He could even smell it—or imagined that he could. He rode back down the slope.

Kate Barringer had already guessed. "The police?"

"And my old friend, Archer," he said coldly, "unless I'm very mistaken. He didn't waste much time getting to the authorities."

"And the fire?"

"Can't be sure at this distance. But I'd guess that Archer and his pals first tried to talk us out of that cave, and when that failed they decided to burn us out. Coal oil, I'd say, poured on the cedars."

She shuddered. "He would do a thing like that, to a friend? For money?"

There were many men now who regarded money as the only real thing left in an unreal world. But Cameron had no wish to dwell on it. "It won't take them long to discover we're not in that cave. I'd like it better if we had more distance between ourselves and that gully."

Shortly before dawn they put the horses into another dry wash, not as deep or protected as the one Archer had selected for them, but it would have to do. They staked the horses and prepared to wait out the day ahead.

In the morning's first light they heard the sound of horsemen quartering southeast across the desert. Cameron and Kate quickly muzzled the horses and kept them silenced until the riders were well past the wash.

Cameron went slightly weak with relief when

he realized that the posse was not going to search their hiding place. They released the horses and studied the retreating backs of the possemen. There were four of them.

"Do you recognize any of them?" he asked.

"Yes." Her face was gray. "Three of them were policemen. Nobodies, like Jamie. The man leading was Blackman."

For a moment Cameron felt as if the ground had been cut away from under him. "Blackman . . ." He pulled his thoughts together and managed a taut smile. "Well, we can forget about Mr. Blackman. Mason or not. I don't think I want to do business with a sheriff's posseman."

The early morning sun seemed particularly savage. The horses stamped nervously as thirst began to nag them. Cameron felt gritty and dirty, and sand lice had already opened a trail to his bristling beard. He and Kate Barringer stared out at the hostile land without any real hope of ever getting out of it. It was going to be a long day.

It was with grim satisfaction and pleasure that William Olive learned that a price had been put on Kate Barringer's head. One hundred dollars.

"True," Gafferty told him, "it ain't nothin' to holler about especially. There's old rebel officers, I hear, that carry as much as a thousand dollars on their heads. Real money. Not

Confederate. But, after all, she's just a woman."

Gafferty, a self-taught dentist who liked to call himself a doctor, looked thoughtfully at Olive's wound. "Lucky that musket ball didn't bust up your shoulder more'n it did. Way things look, you'll be up and around inside a week."

Olive had no intention of spending a week in this miserable huddle of mud huts that called itself Starr. He had been here two days, bedded down on a straw pallet in a livery shed. He had been fed and cared for, after a fashion, but the citizens were beginning to wonder, just a little, about this stranger in their midst. Some thought that a special marshal, as he claimed to be, would be eager to get in touch with Union officials in the district. Instead, Olive had insisted that his presence be kept secret, implying that his mission was too vital to be revealed to mere county officials.

Sheriff Waller had been too busy trying to find the Barringer woman to pay much attention to this mysterious "marshal." But there were others, Doc Gafferty among them, who studied their guest with sidelong glances when they thought Olive wasn't looking. His speech was strange, for one thing, even for a Yankee.

"Now," Gafferty was saying casually as he changed the bandage on Olive's shoulder, "if it had of been the *woman* that shot you, instead of that other feller you mentioned, I reckon the bounty would jump to five hundred at least. After all, can't have folks shootin' down gover'ment marshals."

Gafferty, a soft, sagging man with watery eyes, laughed self-consciously. Olive said, "I expect the sheriff will catch the Barringer woman, in good time." With a curt nod he dismissed the "doctor" and pretended to go to sleep.

He lay perfectly still, breathing slowly, steadily, like a lizard on a warm rock. But his mind was racing. One hundred dollars! As Gafferty had pointed out, it was a long way from a thousand— but one hundred dollars was still an unimaginable fortune to a legionnaire. Also, there was this little matter of a mangled shoulder. Yes sir, he thought coldly, it would be a decided pleasure meeting up with that quick-shooting widow again.

Olive, in his day, had observed many French officers, the young gallants, and the older ones too. They might, without a second thought, send a company of men to certain death, but they would never desert a woman in distress.

This particularly romantic turn of phrase caused Legionnaire Olive to smile in his feigned sleep. Trent had had his own ideas about Cameron, but Olive had seen through the man immediately. The Confederate and the French gallants were cut from the same cloth. Cameron would be duty-bound to look after Kate Barringer. When Olive found one of them, he would find both.

With this satisfying thought in his head, the legionnaire turned on his good side and sank into a real and restful sleep.

It was his third day in Starr as an unofficial guest of the town, and Olive intended it to be his last.

He practiced moving his arm. The shoulder was stiff. The pain at times was bright and shimmering. But, in the *Légion Etrangère*, pain in some form or another was a constant companion. Blister-covered feet filling your boots with blood. The aches of old wounds, or wounds not so old. Savage punishments at the hands of the *sous-officiers*. Refined tortures at the hands of the Berbers. Or, perhaps, only a pain of the mind which in a way was the worst pain of all.

He practiced walking and was pleased to discover that he had lost not too much of his strength. In the Legion he would have been back on active duty twenty-four hours ago. He would have marched forty miles, in greatcoat and full pack, if it had been demanded of him. He wouldn't have dared not to.

He listened to the comings and goings of sheriff's deputies in the main livery barn. There had been a flurry of excitement earlier, but now it was quiet. Only the sluggish gossip of a cow hunter and the stable hand disturbed the silence.

Olive systematically went through the clothing

that he had taken from Trent. He found three double eagles—sixty gold dollars, and a small knife. Olive felt keen disappointment. He had been certain that more money would be found on careful examination of the clothing—in the seams, in the lining, somewhere. But there was no more money. Three double eagles and a bit of silver. Four days ago it would have been a fortune. Now it was hardly a drop in the ocean.

By force of will he made himself calm again. He sighed, and even smiled a little to himself. Anger would not help him. What he needed was a little more rest and some planning. He had no gun, no horse, and little money. But he did have the detective's knife. And he was free of the Legion. That was something. *He was free of the Legion!*

That afternoon Doc Gafferty returned. He was in a sullen mood as he looked at Olive's wound.

"What is it?" Olive asked curiously.

Gafferty shrugged. "The woman, Kate Barringer, escaped the trap the sheriff and his boys set for her. The woman, and a man called Cameron. Old pal of Cameron's out at the hide and tallow works put the sheriff onto them. But like I said, they skedaddled. Deputies been out near two days, beatin' the brush for them."

Olive experienced a dizzying relief. What rotten luck it would have been if that fat ignorant sheriff had captured Cameron and claimed the bounty.

Gafferty said with fake indifference, "This Cameron. He the gent that put the bullet in you?"

Olive did some fast thinking. He didn't want to get himself tangled in too many lies, not at this point, while he still needed the help of these people. He nodded. "Cameron's his name."

The doc grinned. "Nigh thing, wasn't it? Too bad if the sheriff beat you out of your bounty money, after all you been through."

Olive forced a small grin but said nothing.

"But bein' a Yankee marshal and all, I guess you ain't got too much to fret about on that score. Anyhow, it ain't Cameron the sheriff wants. The bounty money . . ." Gafferty shrugged philosophically. "Lawmen can steal more'n that right here in Starr, without takin' chances. But the woman—she's another fish to skin. Can't have women goin' around shootin' gover'ment officials, you know."

The old quack was slowly getting around to something. Impatiently, Olive waited.

Gafferty was elaborately casual. "In the ordinary run of things, the sheriff would be glad to have an expert man-hunter like yourself workin' on his side. Likely he'd be proud to set you up to a good horse and a rifle, and give you Cameron free and clear, when you find him. All he's interested in is the woman."

157

"What makes you think Cameron's going to stay tied up with this woman?"

The doc's grin widened a bit. "For one thing, she's a looker. For another thing, Cameron probably figgers it's the gentlemanly thing to do, to go on lookin' after the lady. And I figger he must be a real old southern gentleman, or he never would of took her with him in the first place."

Olive didn't like the old man's rambling. "What do you want?"

Gafferty laughed. "That's what I like. Get right to the point. I've already got what I want—the five hundred in gold that was sewed in the shoulders of your coat. Took it while you was asleep, of course. Could of took the three double eagles if I'd been a mind to, but I didn't. Don't be greedy, that's my motto."

Olive sat upright, despite the sudden pain. So Trent *had* carried a gold reserve. He studied this slovenly, grinning charlatan with a look that was cold and deadly.

Gafferty regarded the look with indifference. "Thing is," he said pleasantly, "you ain't just the feller you claim to be, and I'm the only one hereabouts that knows it."

Olive's silent rage was more expressive than an angry outburst. It did not worry Gafferty. "I been on the frontier a long time, boy. Long enough to know you ain't no detective from Chicago, or no gover'ment marshal, either. Your talk's all wrong, for one thing. For another thing, your feet. Blisters on blisters, bunions on bunions. Infantry feet. Worst feet I ever seen. Not even old Stonewall Jackson's Valley soldiers had feet bad as yours. No socks. That's the reason. And the French army's the only one I know of that don't issue socks of some kind to their foot soldiers."

The old fool was not quite the fool that Olive had taken him for.

Gafferty sighed. "I don't much like to steal. But a man's got to live. And I'm too old to go raidin' and lootin' with the sheriff's boys. Have to take my livin' where I find it."

"And now that you've found it?" Olive asked in a dull tone.

The old doc shrugged. "Nothin'. I don't owe the sheriff any favors. Don't make any difference to me if you're a French deserter, or if you murdered the real detective somewhere along the line and took his prisoner."

Olive froze. "I don't know what you're talking about."

Gafferty brushed that aside. "Ever'body knows the French've got a renegade outfit they call the Foreign Legion down at Monterrey. Your feet, the whip marks on your back, all the other scars, and the way you talk—it all adds up. Logic, boy. When you get old you got to use logic."

A cold, hard hand twisted Olive's insides.

"Listen to me, boy," Gafferty said seriously. "I need that gold worse than you do. You're young. You've still got a chance to catch Cameron and collect the bounty. Just turn him over to the Yankee authorities. Don't make a damn to them who you are or where you come from."

Having that assurance was, in a way, worth the five hundred. "Has the sheriff given up the search?"

"No help for it." The doc grinned. "The sheriff's Yaqui tracker claims Cameron and the woman struck west, out of the county. Down here, at this particular time, bein' sheriff of a county is like havin' a deed to a gold mine. Dig your own ore any way you please, but leave the other feller's alone."

Olive breathed deeply. "All right," he said evenly. "Keep the gold. But I need a horse, and a repeating rifle and fifty rounds of ammunition."

Gafferty was pleasantly surprised that Olive was taking his loss so sensibly. "The sheriff can arrange it. He still thinks you're some kind of highflyin' Yankee marshal."

"You'll talk to the sheriff?"

"All right, if that's what you want. When do you aim to leave?"

"Today. Anytime after sundown."

Gafferty looked at him in a professional way but said nothing. If he wanted to risk opening the wound again, it was of no particular interest

160

to Gafferty. And, in truth, Starr would likely be a much more peaceful place with this Legion deserter out of it.

After two fruitless days in the desert, an exhausted Sheriff Arvin Waller was sleeping the sleep of the just. Gafferty found him on an army cot in a mud hut that sometimes passed as the county jail. The old doc shook him steadily, patiently, until he came awake.

"I've been talkin' to my patient," Gafferty said. "The one that calls hisself Trent."

The sheriff rubbed his bleary eyes. "*Calls* hisself Trent?"

"I don't know his real name. He's a deserter from the French Army in Mexico. Probably he killed the real Trent and took his outfit. The man he was trailin' when he got shot is the one that's with Kate Barringer."

Now Waller was fully awake, his shrewd brain racing behind a puffy mask. "What does he know about the woman?"

"Not much. At least, I don't think so. His main interest is Cameron and the bounty money."

"Think he can be trusted, this patient of yours?"

Gafferty laughed. "About as far as I could fling a mule by the tail. But he's tough. And he means business. It's my notion that if anybody can catch Cameron, he can."

"And the woman?"

161

"Her, too. If she stays with Cameron."

It was the woman that Waller wanted, captured or killed, he didn't care. Bounty hunting was a game for fools, and a dangerous game at that. Collecting taxes was much more profitable, and safer. But when women started killing your collectors, then action had to be taken. "Maybe I ought to talk to this patient of yours."

Gafferty shook his head. "He's suspicious enough as things stand."

"A man like that—I can't just let him go."

Gafferty looked surprised. "Why not? The Frenchies don't mean nothin' to us, do they?"

To a tired man Gafferty's kind of logic made sense. And Waller was more tired than he had been in a long time. "That woman. If it ever got out that she killed a tax collector and got away with it, none of our hides would be safe. Ever'body would start takin' shots at us."

Gafferty nodded in total agreement. "My notion exactly. And the best way to stop the woman is to let my patient go."

It was almost sundown when Gafferty returned to the shed. Olive was sitting on the edge of his mattress, gently massaging his shoulder.

"The sheriff's a fair man," Gafferty said, with just a hint of dryness. "If he wanted to, he could turn you over to the Yankees, and they'd turn you right back to the French. But he ain't that kind. Look at this." He leaned a slightly battered seven-shot Spencer rifle against the mud wall, then he placed two boxes of rim-fire cartridges at Olive's feet. "First-class rifle, and two boxes of shells, just like you wanted. Out in the street there's a stout little paint bronc waitin' for you." He grinned widely at Olive's look of suspicion. "Doc Gafferty keeps his word, boy. Now I want you to keep yours."

"What about?"

"The woman, boy! The one with Cameron. Dead or alive, she's worth a hundred dollars to the man that brings her in. And just between the two of us, she'd be better off dead. But any way you do it, the bounty's yours. Just knowin' she never got away with killin' a tax collector, that's all the sheriff wants."

Olive gave this a moment of sober thought. It was not as improbable as it would seem at first. Sheriff Waller had a good thing of it here in Starr. And the Barringer woman was in a good way of ruining it.

Obviously Waller was the kind of man to turn bears loose in order to rid himself of foxes. Let those who came after him worry about the bears.

"And that's all there is to it?" Olive asked.

"That's it, boy. Lucky day for you when you run into a man like the sheriff."

Olive was inclined to agree. He got slowly to his feet and went to the door. There at the pole rack was a sturdy, brush-scarred brown and white gelding, saddled and apparently ready to travel.

"What do you say, boy?" Gafferty asked. "Is it a bargain?"

"Bargain?" These Texans had a curious way of putting things. "Yes. It's a bargain. Tell your sheriff there's nothing to worry about—I'll attend to the woman."

Gafferty beamed. "Good! I knowed we could count on you!" No one knew better than Gafferty that the truth was not in men like William Olive. But this time the old doc believed him. There was an unmistakable glint of greed in Olive's eyes.

Doc Gafferty sighed with relief. With an example made of the Barringer woman, the county citizenry could be kept in line for a few months longer.

He came to the door and gazed dreamily out at the dusty street. A few more months. A year, perhaps. By that time he and Waller and the rest of them would have the county picked clean. They would be rich men. With the help of time—and men like William Olive.

It was in a gradual way, not all at once, that Doc Gafferty became aware of the subtle change of atmosphere, a certain chilling of the air, a still and waitful silence. Here was the stillness of an April evening in cyclone country. A hush that was at the same time enervating and depressing.

Little by little, bit by bit, Doc Gafferty became aware of it.

He turned, looked up at Olive, and knew with appalling certainty that he was looking at the face of death itself.

"Old man." Olive's tone was only mildly reproachful. "Old man, after robbing me you should have finished the job and killed me."

Gafferty tried to yell, scream, in some way create a commotion which would bring friends running to his aid. He could not make a sound. His throat was frozen solid. His mouth was dry, his skin like parchment. The tilted point of the knife in Olive's hand held him in a snakelike trance.

Olive killed him where he stood, with the cool indifference of a ritual slaughterer. Gafferty looked startled when the knife went in. He gasped faintly when the knife was withdrawn; a little blood bubbled from the wound, and he fell to the floor.

Unhurriedly, Olive admired the knife for a moment, then he wiped it clean on the dead man's vest and began a meticulous search of the body.

Gafferty had not had Trent's imagination—the gold coins were wrapped in a fold of buckskin and tied about the old man's middle. Olive located them almost immediately. He pocketed the money, stepped over the body, and briefly inspected the rifle and ammunition. The rifle was almost new but had been badly kept. A little oil and some attention to the action would put it right again. Olive picked up the boxes of cartridges and cradled the Spencer in the crook of his arm. Then, for the second time, he stepped over the body of Doc Gafferty and walked out of the shed.

Most of the town was sleeping off the exhaustion of a long and futile hunt for the Barringer woman. The stable hand and a cow hunter sat on a stone water trough in front of the livery barn, watching curiously as Olive went directly to the saddled paint and slowly mounted.

Olive saluted sardonically as he rode past them.

EIGHT

Cameron lay in the shade of a twisted mesquite tree, his hat over his face, wondering what to do next. He didn't know where they were, only that they had almost killed their horses getting there. They were out of food, almost out of water, and the horses would be lucky to last another day without high-energy grain.

"I wonder if that sheriff's posse's still on our trail," he said at last. An idle, stupid question, but these long silences had begun to get on his nerves.

"I doubt it," Kate Barringer said. "But Sheriff Waller's sure to send out some riders to spread the word. He'll send them to the west, because he will know that's the only direction we have open to us." She corrected herself. "Only direction *you* have open. I can strike any direction. That might make it better for both of us. After all, I'm the one they want. You're not important, except to bounty hunters. Nobody around here cares who you might have killed in Louisiana."

He pushed his hat away from his face and looked at her. She lay in the dappled shade, staring up at the lacy mesquite leaves. For the past three days she had been perfectly rational. She had also been of considerable help, for she knew this country and its ways much better than Cameron did. But for the past several hours she had been lost in thought—and Cameron guessed what was in her mind.

"Don't try anything foolish," he told her bluntly. "A woman alone, in this country. You wouldn't last half a day."

She smiled to herself.

"Forget it," he said. "Not just for your own sake, but for mine. I need somebody who knows this land."

"I've never been this far west before. You know the country as well as I do."

"I've never lived in Texas. That makes a difference."

Perhaps that had been the wrong thing to say. Perhaps it had directed her thoughts back to her dead husband and the ranch that he had never had a chance to build. But she only said, "Where do you think we can go from here?"

"The New Mexico country. Maybe Arizona. One thing is certain—no place is safe for us here in the Confederacy. What used to be the Confederacy."

She smiled that faint, secret smile of hers. "Captain, do you know what lies between us and the Territory of New Mexico?"

"Desert, I've heard."

"The Llano Estacado. I've never seen it, but Karl did once. Land so flat and empty of landmarks that even the Indians get lost in it."

"There's the sun," he said. "And the moon and the stars."

"Oh yes," she said with feeling, "there's the sun. And miles of bleaching bones to mark the trail of men who thought to cross the Llano."

They lay for a long while, resting, gathering their strength for another march as soon as night came. Then, when Cameron had thought her asleep, Kate Barringer said, "Do you know what I am afraid of? Not the Llano. Not Sheriff Waller's posse, or any of the other posses that he probably has alerted. Not even the possibility of starving, or dying of thirst. No—the only thing I'm truly afraid of is the man who brought you to my 'dobe. The one I shot."

Cameron looked at her but said nothing. A thought very similar to hers had been going through his own mind. "Olive?" he asked, as if the thought was mildly amusing. "A musket ball in his shoulder, it'll be a long while before he goes man hunting."

She closed her eyes. "I have the feeling that Mr. Olive is not the sort to pay much attention to wounded shoulders, not even his own."

That night they rode north, generally parallel to the Bravo. They struck a sluggish river, the Nueces, tasted its bitter water, and continued on to the north.

169

The brush country was grudgingly giving way to rocky hills and prairie. Cameron dredged his memory for odd facts of geography that he had learned once at the private academy at Ayersville.

Bearing west they would strike the old territory of Bexar, an extension of the Llano, the beginning of the High Plains. Still farther west was the Pecos River, the big bend of the Rio Bravo Del Norte, mountains, basins, wilderness, all crosshatched by Comanche war trails still very much in use. North of the Pecos was the Llano proper, and west of that, New Mexico.

Early that morning they chased a rabbit into a hollow log and twisted it out with a stick and killed it. Not even in this land that seemed totally deserted did Cameron wish to risk firing the Henry. But the rabbit was wormy. Better to go hungry.

Later Cameron killed a turkey gobbler roosting in a cottonwood, this time with the rifle. They cooked the turkey over a spare fire on the bank of the Pecos and washed it down with bitter water. With a full belly and something to drink and a chance to rest, Cameron began to feel more hopeful.

Ahead of them lay the great limestone tablelands and the deserts of granite and sandstone. This was Comanche land, and the Indians were feeling strong and cocky now that the white soldiers had wasted themselves in their own war.

But it was not the Indians that bothered Cameron. He knew that a man like Waller, in his own insidious way, was more dangerous than a whole party of Comanches. And William Olive, with ruthlessness and courage and skill to support his money hunger, was more dangerous than either.

Kate Barringer said, "The old Presidio Roads can't be far north of here. There's a family, friends of Karl's, that live close by, on Turkey River."

His experience with Archer had jaded Cameron's fondness for old friends. "I think we'll do better by ourselves."

She was silent for a moment. "I was thinking of myself. I'm tired. I don't think I can make it across the Bexar, much less the Llano. Leave me on the Turkey, the Bernsons will look after me until the time real law comes to Texas."

She was offering him escape, freeing him of the necessity of burdening himself with a woman. Cameron was dismayed to find that the prospect of such freedom was almost irresistible. He could travel much faster alone, arouse less suspicion.

She sensed his brief struggle. The new order of self-preservation against the old outmoded code of honor. She smiled. "You've done all you can for me, Captain. And like I said, I'm too tired to go much farther."

". . . Tell me about these Bernsons."

She shrugged. "A family my husband met when he was hunting cattle. They used to operate a swing station on the stage road to El Paso."

He shook his head. "I don't like it."

"The man, Ike Bernson, owes Karl for livestock that he bought before the war. He'll be glad enough to settle the debt by putting me up for a while."

"You never saw these people. You don't know what they're like."

"Honest and hard working, my husband said."

Cameron thought of his old friend Archer. "Four years of war can change a man." The morning sun was dazzling, unbelievably hot. "Get some rest," he said. "We'll talk about it later."

From a shaggy crest bristling with prickly pear and needle grass, William Olive studied the terrain before him. He scanned it methodically, professionally, with slitted eyes. What he saw was a sea of bunch grass and cactus, with an occasional wash fringed with the water-sapping plague of salt cedar.

This was what the Americans called a desert. Olive could have laughed. He had seen deserts that would make this one look like the sweetest corner of paradise.

He was dehydrated and hungry, and the gyp water that he had drunk that morning had turned his stomach slightly sickish—but that too was laughable to a man who had lived for weeks on water sucked from mudholes and tasting of camel urine. There was some pain in his shoulder, but all things considered, William Olive felt himself in good condition.

With reasonable luck, he estimated that he would have Cameron recaptured within another two days. Three at the most. That he could possibly fail to capture Cameron did not once enter his mind, for he was certain now that Cameron and the woman were traveling together.

Shining coins had miraculously stimulated memories along the way. An old tanner at the hide and tallow plant had seen Cameron and the Barringer woman ride off together. But he hated tax collectors and had said nothing to the sheriff's men. A cow hunter had glimpsed the pair not far from the Lower Presidio Road and was making for the sheriff's office in Starr when Olive intercepted him. Hard luck for the cow hunter. It had been necessary to kill him.

Now he was somewhere north of the Upper Presidio, and all his instincts told him that the chase was nearing its end.

The day before he had discovered the ashes of a campfire and the stripped bones of a turkey. He searched the ground around the dead ashes and was generously rewarded. Among the faint footprints was a set that could only have been made by a woman.

He had also noted that their blankets had been thrown against rocks that shielded them from the sun. So they were probably traveling nights and sleeping days.

Olive traveled days, pushing the rugged little paint as hard as he dared. Now he sensed that he was near his prey. The game was almost won. He rode on to the north, toward the El Paso Road and the territory still known to some as Bexar.

He traveled through the hot afternoon, across the waterless plains. Suddenly the trail ended. For hours he had been following a trail that was almost recklessly clear, followed it into some old adobe ruins beside a dried-up stream, and there it had ended.

The baked clay along the dry wash was hard as the hard-pan that he had noticed before along certain bluffs. But not so hard that shod horses wouldn't have left some kind of trace.

He looked for drag signs, but there were none. Olive felt the paint trembling with fatigue, but that did not worry him. He had no more feeling for horses than he had for men. At last he climbed down to inspect the area more closely. He almost fell to his knees.

He was dismayed to discover that his legs were rubbery, his breathing shallow and fluttering. His eyes no longer focused with needle-like sharpness. How long had he gone without food and water? As long as the paint—and that rugged little animal was almost done for.

This was something to think about. He tied the paint to a runted mesquite, then he sat with his back against the crumbling adobe wall. Obviously, he had been so intent on overtaking Cameron and the Barringer woman that he had overtaxed himself. His mouth was as dry as powder. The shoulder wound was a smoldering fire that was slowly spreading up one side of his neck and down his arm.

This was not the first time that he had been thirsty, hungry, exhausted, and in pain—perhaps that was the reason he had not paid much attention to his condition.

Olive looked bleakly at the paint. The animal stood hip-shot, head down, too tired even to eat the pale green leaves of the mesquite. He knew that the horse needed water and something solid in its belly, but then, so did Olive. At the moment there was nothing he could do about either of them.

He tried to concentrate on the vanished trail. After all, he was a legionnaire, he had tracked wily Arab tribesmen over deserts many times more desolate than this one. There was a reasonable answer. He had only to apply himself and it would come to him. But even as he thought it, his head was drooping. In another minute he was sleeping.

When he awoke, the paint was down. Olive

did not immediately appreciate the significance of this. Camels knelt or sprawled in the sand to sleep, so the paint must be sleeping.

Olive took careful inventory of his own condition. He noted that his skin felt drawn and overly sensitive—this meant fever. His tongue lay like a dead, dry thing in his mouth. With military objectiveness, he estimated that he could last another twelve hours without water, provided he kept to the shade and did nothing to hasten the process of evaporation.

This did not worry him particularly, for he had marched and fought in worse conditions than this. Except for his wounded shoulder, which was now a thing of fire. He had given Doc Gafferty too much credit, too soon. He knew without looking that the wound was infected.

The thing that irritated and vaguely angered him was his own stupidity. This, he lectured himself, is what comes of being greedy, of thinking only of Cameron and the bounty, when he should have given some thought to himself.

The thing to do, he knew, was rest, gather his strength, then go looking for water and food. And do whatever possible about the infected wound.

He tried not to think about that spreading fire in his shoulder. Thinking of the wound led to thinking about the Barringer woman and this in turn would, sooner or later, lead to blind, reasonless anger.

This was not the time for anger. Just the same, he made up his mind that he would not turn the woman over to the authorities. The hundred dollars was not that important now. In the back of his feverish mind he was beginning to develop some ideas on how best to deal with Kate Barringer.

Until now he hadn't really noticed that night had come while he slept. A white moon shone down on the wasteland, and he could smell the tantalizing sweetness of moisture in the air, moisture brought in on the south wind from the Gulf of Mexico.

Olive spread a blanket to trap the early morning dew. Tomorrow he would find water. He had already crossed several streams, some dry, some mere trickles, but water beds at least. He would dig in these beds, if he had to, and find water. But he doubted that such measures would be necessary. This was not the Sahara.

Shortly before dawn he tested the blanket and found it damp. With loving care he used the knife to scrape together the few drops of moisture, and he licked it up with his dry tongue.

The paint was still down. The animal stared at Olive with wall eyes and made disturbing noises, deep in its chest. There was a delicate pinkish froth about the horse's muzzle—Olive noticed this for the first time.

He pulled on the paint's headstall. It hadn't occurred to him to unsaddle, or even to unbit the animal before tying it to the mesquite. The paint didn't get up. More froth appeared on its muzzle, and there was a certain glaze in those big eyes. Olive realized now that the horse was dying. Killing it cleanly, quickly, with a bullet, would have been the merciful thing to do. But they didn't teach mercy in the Legion.

Olive rested some more and began to change his plans, oblivious to those big eyes watching him sadly. The first signs of dawn cleared the eastern horizon. He would have to start moving soon, while it was still cool.

He took his Spencer from the saddle scabbard, pocketed the two boxes of ammunition, and began walking. He could feel his strength leaving him. But in the Legion, when strength was gone a man learned to fight on nerve, or fear, or hate. Or simply because he was a legionnaire.

Olive came across a thicket of prickly pear and remembered that he had seen wild cattle eating the small red fruits on which golden blossoms were set. He cut some of the fruits, peeled them and ate them. They were surprisingly good, cool and sweet. He sat down and ate them thoughtfully, until his constricted stomach began to rebel. He chewed a few more for the liquid content and spat out the pulp.

He rested awhile and felt better, stronger. Perhaps it was the sugar content in the fruit, like the sweet black grapes of Algeria.

He walked on. From time to time he would cut one of the small red "apples" from the prickly pear and suck the juice. The juices soon relaxed his knotted stomach, and he began to hunger for more solid food.

Walking in a half daze, more or less aimlessly, he searched for signs of Cameron and the woman. His shoulder continued to pain him, but he had nothing to treat it with. He did not remove the dirty bandage to look at the wound. He knew what gangrene in its early stages looked like.

The sun was dazzling and cruel, but not so cruel as the sun of central Algeria. He walked on. At times when he stumbled, the thought of Cameron and the thousand-dollar bounty kept him going. And Kate Barringer and the sweet thought of revenge.

Olive was sitting on a limestone outcrop, getting his breath and gingerly rubbing his fiery shoulder, when he saw the horsebacker riding out of the savage sun.

He watched them, man and horse appearing as one in the distance. A quiet, cold thought moved through Olive's mind. He stood up and waved his rifle to attract the rider's attention. The horsebacker saw him, hesitated, then reined toward him. Olive carefully checked the action on the Spencer.

The rider was a small, florid man in his middle years. And he was angry.

179

"You the one that went off and left that paint to die by itself in the sun?"

It took a few seconds for Olive to understand his anger. "The horse was done for. Nothing I could have done for it. Do you have any water?"

The rider's mouth turned down. But he handed Olive a hemp-covered canteen. Olive drank slowly, carefully, savoring every drop of the hot, mineral-tasting water. He felt the juices of life flowing down his throat and into his stomach. He drank as much as he dared—more now would have made him sick. Reluctantly, he capped the canteen and handed it back to the rider. Only then did Olive notice the deputy's badge pinned over the rider's vest pocket.

He did not look like a lawman. The man's hands were gnarled and calloused, a laborer's hands. And Olive recognized some of his own awkwardness in the man, in the way he sat his saddle and wore his clothes. Both saddle and riding dress were obviously strange to him.

Olive had him pegged. The man was merely another of the many incompetents that the present masters of the South had enlisted as sheriff's deputies. Misfits, like the slow-witted Jamie, whose life Kate Barringer had spared. A silent thought was taking shape in Olive's mind. He did not think that this deputy would be as lucky as Jamie.

The rider noticed Olive's interest in the badge. He sat a little straighter. "Deputy Mallard," he said with dignity. "Ridin' for Sheriff Matthews over at . . ." He shot Olive a sidelong look and changed the subject. "Don't reckon you seen anything of a woman horsebacker, did you?"

"Woman?"

The deputy nodded importantly. "Name of Barringer. Shot a gover'ment man down by Starr somewheres. Got word on the telegraph wire just this mornin'."

Mallard shrewedly refrained from mentioning the bounty. Olive smiled faintly, his mind racing. Apparently Cameron and the woman had succeeded in escaping Sheriff Waller's men. Now they were in another county with a new set of lawmen after them. But, by special riders and by telegraph, Waller had managed to spread the word.

The deputy shifted uneasily in the saddle. He did not like the quiet, possessive way that Olive was looking at his horse.

"This woman you're looking for," Olive said. "I wouldn't think she'd get far, by herself."

"Ain't by herself, accordin' to the sheriff in Starr. Might be runnin' with a hardcase from Louisiana."

Again he cannily refrained from mentioning the bounty. Olive sighed. The world, it seemed, was filled with fools. But Mallard had confirmed his own conviction that Cameron and the Barringer woman were traveling together. For that frail piece of information, Olive was grateful.

But not grateful enough to hesitate shooting the deputy. In a casual, almost bored, way he simply raised the muzzle of the Spencer and fired from the hip.

The claybank, startled by the explosion, reared abruptly. Mallard, even more startled than the horse, was partially lifted from the saddle by the bullet's impact. He grabbed frantically for the saddle horn, missed, and began to fall. Olive grabbed the animal's chain bit and curbed it brutally.

The deputy struck the ground solidly, moaning, struggling in a hopeless way to hold back a fearful darkness. Mallard was well along the road to death, but Olive did not bother to watch his leaving. Instead, he led the horse away from the smell of blood and tied the reins to a mesquite trunk.

Methodically, he investigated the saddle pockets and the saddle roll, taking only what he needed. Tobacco, a small packet of salt, another packet of jerked beef, a few sourdough biscuits, stale and as hard as bullets. He took a box of .52 caliber cartridges but left the rifle. The weapon was a Confederate copy of the Spencer, poorly made and with a pitted barrel. Along with the canteen, he set aside his small bonanza and returned to Mallard.

By this time the deputy was dead. Olive turned him over and went through his pockets. There was a printed description of Kate Barringer and a notice of the reward. A fast job of printing. The new masters of the South must want her very much.

Olive kept the poster, took some matches and the few silver coins that Mallard had been carrying. That ended his interest in Deputy Mallard, a man who should have stuck to honest labor and ignored the siren call of the scalawag police.

The former member of the *Légion Etrangère* rested for a moment and took stock of the situation. He knew in a vague way that Cameron must necessarily travel a narrow corridor between the river boundary of Mexico and the Union authorities to the north. He would be aiming for one of the neutral territories to the west, New Mexico or Arizona.

For the first time since the killing of Sergent-Chef Ciano, William Olive experienced a growing sensation of urgency. He did not doubt his own talents; on the other hand he could not ignore the insidious effects of a seriously infected wound. In a coldly professional way, he calculated the odds. Without competent medical attention, such an infection might well kill him within a week.

Again he began to add his chances, figure his

odds. The pain did not unduly concern him, but the fever did. High fever meant a fuzzy mind; a man began to see things that were not real, hear things that were only in his head. The *cafard* of the dying.

But, with food in his belly and water to cool his insides, he decided that he would have two days left, possibly three. Two days of reasonably clear and objective thinking. Two days in which to pick up the lost trail, to find Cameron and the woman, and report to the proper authorities for his bounty.

Olive studied the deep-barreled claybank with a thoughtful eye. He went to the animal, stroked the quivering withers without affection. He climbed slowly into the saddle.

The deputy's brackish water had relieved Olive's gritty throat and cooled his brain. He could see the insanity of blundering aimlessly in a strange desert. He would have to go back and start again, no matter how much precious time it might cost him.

He returned to that crumbling adobe hut, then to the dead campsite, the turkey bones, the lip of hardpan along the wash. It was the same as before. Not as much as a single dint in that rocklike crust. Still, he knew that shod horses had to leave some kind of trace, even on stone.

He followed that strip of sun-baked earth where nothing grew, for he was sure that, trace or no trace, this was the way that Cameron had traveled. He got down and led the claybank, searching the ground with angry eyes. He was squandering strength that he should have been hoarding—but in the end he was rewarded.

Something foreign caught his eye, something that smacked of "man" in this almost manless wilderness of gravel and thornbrush. It had been stuffed into what appeared to be an abandoned coyote hole. But a ground squirrel or some other wild creature had managed to work part of it out.

What he had found was the tattered, hard-used remains of hemp sacking. Cameron had simply wrapped the hooves of their horses with the sacking. That explained the absence of tracks.

Still leading the claybank, Olive soon rediscovered the trail. A snapped twig of mesquite. Crushed young grass that had not yet rejuvenated itself. Animal droppings.

Olive felt better than he had for days. Suddenly he threw his head back and laughed.

He drank some of the blood-warm water from the deputy's canteen. He rested for a little while and tried not to think about his shoulder. Soon it would be over. He had the trail again, and this time he would not lose it. They were not traveling fast, the woman holding Cameron back like the iron ball on a prisoner's leg.

Olive smiled. One more day, with any kind of luck. And it would all be over.

NINE

Cameron came awake slowly. He felt heavy and sluggish, and soured on the inside. Beneath the big mesquite tree, where they had thrown their blankets, the shade had moved, and the sun had burned a fiery brand across one side of his face.

The sun was still more than an hour high, but impatience gnawed at him. They were a long way from Starr, and he now considered sheriffs' posses only a vague threat. But Legionnaire William Olive was another proposition altogether.

It had seemed a wonderful stroke of luck when he found the pile of rotten sacking at the adobe. He had been so sure that a Foreign Legionnaire would know nothing of the old Comanche trick of hoof-wrapping. Now he wasn't so sure. The sacking had worn out too quickly. . . .

He made himself stop thinking about the legionnaire. He turned his thoughts in another direction, toward New Mexico.

The call of the western territories was like a siren song in his mind. Liveoak, Ayersville—he knew that he would never see them again. Like a lot of other lost men in that summer of 1865, he had begun to accept the fact that he was lost. And it was highly unlikely that he would ever find himself in the past.

Without opening his eyes, he said, "Kate, maybe we ought to get started. We're far enough from Starr—I don't think the sheriff's bunch will venture this far. We can risk traveling a little by daylight."

Somewhere along the line he had stopped calling her Mrs. Barringer. Not much time now for proper introductions and cautious cultivation of friendships.

After a moment he said again, "Kate . . ."

This time he sat up and looked at the place nearby where she had been sleeping. She was not there. Nothing of hers was there. Cameron got to his feet, suddenly chilled.

He rubbed weariness from his face, shook fog from his brain. Her horse was not in the draw where it had been staked. Kate Barringer was gone. Cameron returned to the mesquite where he had stacked his riding gear. It was then that he noticed the bit of cardboard, part of a cartridge box, wrapped around the saddle horn. There was a note, brief and blunt, written with a lead bullet.

Thanks, it said. *I'll be all right with the Bernsons.*

That was all. Cameron stared at it. His first sensation was one of overwhelming relief. He felt suddenly light and free, as if he had been relieved of a heavy load. At last he was free to travel as fast as possible, with no thought of pacing himself on a woman's account.

He brought the dun up from the draw and got it saddled. For a moment he shielded his eyes against the westering sun and thought, three days will see me out of Texas. He could understand the excitement that must have driven the old Israelites when they had neared the Promised Land.

The business of wrapping the hooves of the horses had been a child's game, of course—it wouldn't take Olive long to see through that and get back on the trail. But a man traveling alone, on a good horse, should have little trouble staying ahead of a wounded legionnaire in a strange land.

It was all very pleasant to think about. Except for one thing. He couldn't do it.

He knew it the moment he climbed into the saddle. Kate's friends, the Bernsons—Cameron didn't even know if they were alive. Perhaps they were the creations of a confused mind. Or possibly Kate had known all along that no such family existed. He had seen the concern in her face. She had known that she was holding him back, making his escape more difficult.

Cameron sighed and accepted the inevitable.

As long as there was light, her trail was not difficult to follow. He finally arrived at a poisonous little stream tasting wildly of iron and gypsum.

This, on the edge of the Bexar, was what they called a river. Turkey River.

The lingering twilight gave way to stark prairie darkness. Soon a hard, white moon appeared and Cameron continued on for a cautious mile or so. A pale, small light shone weakly in the distance.

Cameron reined up, considered, and then approached the light warily.

It was a cabin of some sort, standing on a barren slope on the other side of the river. The Bernson place? A headquarters shack for cow hunters? An abandoned hut that some traveler was using for the night?

A sheriff's deputy, maybe? A convention of sheriff's deputies, for all Cameron knew.

If he wanted to be sure, he'd have to move in closer. He drew the rifle from the saddle boot and kneed the dun across the shallow stream.

Nothing larger than prickly pear grew on that rocky slope. Cameron felt uncomfortably naked as he approached the cabin.

With a rifleman's eye, Cameron judged the distance between himself and the cabin to be one hundred yards. He moved in a little closer and called, "Kate!"

The light went out.

A rifle crashed. Cameron felt the hot breath of the bullet as it burned past his head. The dun, spooked by the rifle fire, reared and all but dumped Cameron from the saddle. The rifle in the cabin crashed again.

In a land where horses were as necessary to life as food and water, they were protected as much as possible. "Light out!" Cameron barked, giving the animal a kick as he rolled out of the saddle.

Cameron hit the sun-baked ground with his shoulder, rolling awkwardly in the gravel. At last he rolled to a stop behind a clump of prickly pear, the breath knocked out of him, his shoulder numb. He looked up in time to see the dun spurting across the slope, away from the cabin. It was a sight that Cameron viewed with mixed emotions. He thought, I'll catch him later. I hope.

Now the cabin was silent. A sagging shack against a lifeless backdrop of gravel and cactus. The moon, once bright, was now withdrawn, indifferent, distant. Cameron got his breath and ran his hand over the Henry's action. The rifle seemed to be all right. He turned his attention exclusively to the cabin.

Was this the Bernson place? Karl Barringer's good friends, the family that he had befriended, the people that Kate Barringer was depending on for help?

A certain itchiness of the scalp, an indescribable cooling of the blood, told Cameron that he had hit it. Kate Barringer was in the cabin. He had to take that as solid fact. She was probably a prisoner of her husband's good and trusted friends. Suddenly

Cameron knew these Bernsons as though they had been his own friends. He could see their eyes, dull with failure. Their mouths turned down, as if they had tasted life and found it bitter. He knew their craftiness, bolstered by cunning and greed.

Oh yes, Cameron thought, he knew their kind. He had seen enough of them since the war. And any way you took them, they were dangerous.

"Cameron!"

The voice was high pitched and dryly gleeful. They know my name, Cameron thought. Kate has to be in the cabin with them. How else could they have known, or guessed, that I'd be alone?

"Might as well talk up," the disembodied voice was saying. "We got your woman. And Billy's patience is wore plumb thin. Wouldn't surprise me if he put a bullet right in her gizzard, 'less you talk up'n do like I say."

Cameron drew in a long breath. His muscles felt limp, his brain numb. "What do you want?"

The voice cackled. It was an old man's voice. "Stand up and walk towards the cabin. Nice and easy. No guns. You come and see your woman, then we'll talk business."

He couldn't even be sure that Kate was alive. Dead or alive; the bounty could be collected either way. "Let me talk to Kate."

There was a moment of hesitation. Then, with a shrug in his voice, the old man said, "Let her say something, Billy."

There was another stretch of silence. Then a second voice was heard, ill-tempered and shrill, almost girlish. "Talk up! Like Pa says!"

Cameron waited. Seconds crawled like hours. Finally the old man drawled, "Looks like she don't want to say nothin'. Billy . . ."

A thin scream cut the night like bright steel. A fury that Cameron could not control jerked him to his feet.

The old man said dryly, "Just set your rifle down, mister."

Cameron was trembling. He was gripping the Henry so hard that his arms ached. Still, he had no choice. Very slowly, taking it one step at a time, he put the rifle down, he unclinched his fists, and he started toward the cabin.

The old man said, "Ma, you watch the woman. Billy, go out and see how he's fixed." He waited until Cameron was about twenty feet from the cabin's sagging front porch and then said, "Woah," and Cameron stopped.

Ike Bernson, a frail, weary, sapless little man, stepped outside, a rifle pointed at Cameron's middle. Billy, twice the size of his father, with a small, soft mouth and peach-bloom cheeks, scurried around the old man and screamed, "Don't you move, mister! Stand right still, 'less'n I say different!"

This, Cameron guessed, was Billy, whose normal emotional state was near-hysteria and whose normal voice was an unpleasant compromise between a whine and a scream. Now, half-crouched, suspicious as a lobo wolf, he waved a heavy old cap and ball pistol in Cameron's face. Cameron obligingly opened his coat to show that he had no revolver. Billy's face darkened with disappointment. Then it brightened. "Pa, can I have the rifle?"

"Later," Ike Bernson said. "Get him in the house and let's have a look at him."

Billy headed Cameron onto the creaking porch and into the shack. Ike struck a match and relit the lamp—his face, in the hard-edged light, grinned like a death's-head.

For the moment Cameron did not look at Billy or his father. He was dimly aware of the soiled, crumpled heap of a woman, rocking monotonously in a much-repaired, wired-together rocking chair. In her bony hands was an ancient but deadly-looking scatter-gun, and its muzzle was only inches from Kate Barringer's face.

Kate sat very straight, her hands bound behind her, in the only other chair in the room. She looked at Cameron with wide, tired eyes, a look that said, you fool, why didn't you get out of Texas while you had the chance! On her left cheek was a yellowish bruise that would soon be black and purple, something to remember Billy by, no doubt.

"Are you all right?"

193

She nodded heavily, too exhausted or too shocked or too numb to speak.

"These are the friends you told me about?" he couldn't help asking. "The Bernsons?"

She nodded again. "They know everything. About both of us. The tax collector, the bounty money, everything."

"How?"

"I told them. I know, I shouldn't have. I should have remembered your friend at Bellah's Post Office. But it didn't seem like the same thing. These people . . ." She glanced at Ike and Billy and the old woman. Whatever she felt toward them, it was too profound to be shaped in surface emotions such as anger. "These people. I thought they were friends of Karl's."

The old man cackled. Billy giggled like a young girl. "Folks change," Ike said, nodding wisely.

Kate looked at him with no show of emotion.

Billy giggled again, but the old man was ready to get down to business. "Get some rope, Billy. Tie up that fancy army man. Then you get the black mule saddled and ride into Rock Crossin'. Tell the sheriff to start countin' out the bounty, we got the one called Cameron, and the woman with him."

Billy left the cabin, still giggling. Ike stood grinning, his rifle slung carelessly in the crook of his arm. He knew that he didn't have to worry about any sudden moves from this former officer and gentleman of the Confederacy—not as long as the old woman held the scatter-gun in Kate's face.

Cameron looked to Kate for some sort of help. She had been their prisoner for several hours now; she must have noticed something that could help them, some kind of chink in the Bernson armor.

But her eyes had gone strangely vacant again. They waited. Ike grinned, thinking no doubt of the fortune that would soon be his. The old woman sat dull-eyed, rocking, rocking, the muzzle of the scatter-gun moving like a pendulum back and forth in front of Kate's face.

At last Billy returned with a coil of rusty haywire. "Couldn't find no rope."

"Wire'll do." Ike gestured impatiently. "Bind up his hands. Then set him in the corner and fix his feet. Prize rooster like that one, don't want him to fly to coop."

Billy thought this was very funny. He giggled all the time that he bound Cameron's hands behind his back. He then shoved Cameron down in a corner of the shack and wired his feet together. Billy eyed Cameron's silver cavalry spurs. "Can I have them, Pa?"

"Later. You can have the spurs, boots, everything. But there'll be time for that after you come back with the deputies."

Reluctantly, Billy left his prisoner booted and spurred for the present.

Ike picked his teeth with a pocketknife and grinned amiably at his prisoners. After a while he glanced at his wife. "Watch out, old woman." He went out into the yard and came back with the Henry. He leaned his own heavy, outdated weapon against the wall and admired the Henry for some time. His grin widened. Soon he'd be able to buy all the Henries he wanted. He'd be rich. He could buy anything he pleased.

Cameron felt his hands going cold and lifeless. The wire bit into his wrists as he strained against the ungiving wire. For a little while he could feel warm blood crawling down his fingers, but after a time he could not even feel that. At last he looked at Kate and asked, "How far is it to Rock Crossing?"

She shook her head. "I don't know. This country is strange to me."

But the people were even stranger. No great battles had been fought here in Texas. There had been few large slave-owners. Many Texans had voted for secession and war more in the spirit of adventure than for any Confederate cause. But the great adventure had soured. Men like Sheriff Waller and his deputies, and men like Ike Bernson, resented the demands that the war had made on them. But at the moment Ike Bernson was thinking that maybe the war hadn't been such a bad idea after all. Without the war there would have been no Cameron or Kate Barringer. There would have been no bounty.

Cameron clinched his jaws and sawed his wrists against the wire that cut like knives. Good hemp rope, securely knotted, he knew to be as unyielding as a prison wall. Wire was something else. With time and exposure, metal lost some of its strength. It became rigid, like the joints of an old man. It became brittle when drawn into slender strands such as haywire. It broke easily.

But the wire on his wrists did not break easily. It did not break at all. He sawed, working his wrists back and forth. Ike Bernson looked at him with dim amusement. He knew what Cameron was doing. He didn't care. He had personally supervised the binding of the wrists, and he was not worried.

Ike yawned widely. He was sleepy, but not so sleepy that he would leave the prisoners in the sole care of his wife. He stepped outside and glanced at the stars. He came back smiling.

"First light in about three hours. Billy ought to be back by then, with the deputies."

He spoke to no one in particular, and no one bothered to comment. Cameron sawed relentlessly, blindly, on the wire. The old man grinned. He went to the kitchen safe, found a red-jacketed potato and began to peel it with his pocketknife.

He peeled it carefully, the thin paring coiling down and away in one piece from the white meat of the potato. When the job was expertly done, Ike cast the long paring out the door, cut himself a slice of raw potato, and ate it slowly.

Cameron did not look at Kate but he sensed that she was watching him, aware of what he was doing, or trying to do. Don't cause yourself so much pain, she seemed to be saying. When it's so hopeless.

Cameron, his hands numb as wooden stumps, continued his sawing, wondering dimly if he were injuring himself permanently.

Permanently. With a thousand-dollar bounty on your head, the word didn't have much meaning.

Time passed with nightmarish slowness. Ike Bernson had finished his potato and was now using the knife to pare his nails. And then, quite suddenly, the wire on Cameron's wrists snapped.

The suddenness of it took him by surprise. Blood resumed circulation in his hands, feeling returned. He felt the spreading network of fire in each finger. Finally he could feel the warm wetness of his own blood.

He shot a look at Ike Bernson, but apparently the old man had noticed nothing. Cameron took a deep breath and slowly began to topple over on his left side.

It was not difficult to pretend that unconsciousness was slowly pulling him under. The sudden release of the wires had left him strangely dizzy. Ike Bernson grunted with surprise.

Kate Barringer was suddenly alert. "Help him!" she said angrily to the old man. "Can't you see he's hurt?"

"Hurt?" Bernson was honestly puzzled.

"The wires on his wrists. Billy made them too tight." Her voice was harsh and edged with disgust. "Isn't it enough for you, turning the widow of a friend in for bounty? Do you have to have torture as well?"

Bernson cocked his head. He hadn't thought of it as torture, he simply hadn't wanted to risk losing so valuable a prisoner. He glanced at his wife. "Take a look at him."

"Why?" the old woman asked dully, without interrupting her ceaseless rocking. "Dead or alive, the deputies said. What difference does it make?"

"It might just be," her husband said slyly, "that it ain't the wires at all. It could be the plague, for all we know."

Kate saw the old woman's eyes sharpen. Plague was something she understood. This wouldn't be the first time she had seen a person keel over for no reason at all. The next thing you knew, whole settlements, whole towns, were keeling over. She lowered the scatter-gun and started to get up from the rocker.

Then she grinned with toothless cunning. "You

199

can look at him yourself, if it's the plague."

"I never said it was the plague," Ike snapped in irritation. "Just that it *could* be."

It was all the same to the old woman.

Her husband scowled in indecision. He knew it was foolish, but he didn't like the way Kate Barringer was looking at him. He was secure in the knowledge that he was well inside the law; she was the one on the outside. What he was doing was what any law-abiding man would do, never mind the bounty. That was what he wanted to think. But the way the woman looked at him, the disgust in her eyes . . . Ike Bernson sighed.

Cameron was waiting, and praying. Let him come closer. Just a little closer. Ike Bernson obligingly folded his pocketknife and shuffled forward.

With more curiosity than mercy, the old man bent over to look at Cameron's hands. Cameron gathered himself. Suddenly he kicked with both feet, slamming the heels of his worn cavalry boots into the old man's middle.

Ike Bernson grunted in pain and surprise. Cameron had tricked him! It wasn't fair, using a man's better nature to play tricks on him! A sense of outrage showed plainly in Bernson's wrinkled face, even as he stumbled across the floor and fell against the cabin wall. Try to help somebody, the expression said bitterly, and this is what happens!

Only for an instant did Cameron dwell on the

old man's indignation. The danger now lay in the hands of the stone-faced old woman in the rocker. He lurched to his knees and tried to throw himself at her, but the wire on his ankles caused him to fall awkwardly on his face. He tried to break the fall with his hands and was appalled to discover that they were almost useless.

As in a nightmare, he watched the old woman recover from her fear of plagues. There were no mysteries about her, all her thoughts, when she had any, were written in her leathery face and in those dull eyes. Now Cameron was reading satisfaction. He had the chill impression that she wanted to smile but had forgotten how. A lot of nonsense, the expression was saying, listening to her husband all this time. Right this minute she could be in bed sleeping, resting, perhaps even dreaming of the good days and good times before her husband had brought her to this hated place called Texas, if they had killed the two prisoners in the beginning, the way she had wanted.

Talk of plague had rattled her for a moment— she had lost her girl baby to the plague, her father to cholera, her mother to milk fever. She watched unfeeling as Ike reeled across the room and smashed into the wall. Served him right for not listening to her.

The muzzle of the scatter-gun, which she had held for so long in the Barringer woman's face, now drooped toward the floor. No matter. The man called Cameron was no immediate threat. The woman's wrists were still bound firmly with wire. Plenty of time to lift the muzzle and pull the trigger.

From the corner of his eye Cameron glimpsed another movement. Kate Barringer twisting in her chair, hurling herself across the old woman's lap, across the long barrel of the scatter-gun. The frail rocker splintered. Kate and the old woman crashed to the floor, the old woman clawing animal-like for the weapon that had been knocked from her hands.

Cameron lurched forward and threw himself across the barrel. Hissing, dark gums gleaming wetly between curled lips, Mrs. Bernson fought savagely to recover the gun. Cameron, his hands clumsily obeying the commands of his brain, dragged the weapon away from her grasp.

He spoke sharply to Kate. "Move to one side. Out of the way."

Her hands were still bound. She had to roll on the floor until she was out of the line of fire. In a rage the old woman knocked her head on the floor; she made thin, savage little sounds of frustration and despair. Ike Bernson, the breath still knocked out of him, was indifferent to the moment of violence. He sagged gray-faced against the wall, gasping for air.

TEN

Legionnaire William Olive sat with his back to the sun, observing the scene before him with professional interest. He had staked the claybank on the sun side of a slope, and for some time had been crouching here in a mesquite thicket, observing the shack and the activity around it.

There were eight horses tied in thornbush beside the shack. Heavily armed men tramped about with aimless pomposity, the sure mark of green soldiers or amateur lawmen.

There had been many loud and blustery conversations between the deputies and an old man and old woman. An overgrown, excitable youth rushed from one person to another, shouting in a high-pitched voice and waving his arms, but no one seemed to pay any attention.

With effort, Olive curbed his irritation. The deputies, in their stupidity, had trampled down any trace that Cameron and the woman might have left behind them. There was not the slightest doubt in his mind that Cameron and the Barringer woman were the cause of all the excitement.

He had followed their trail along the creek bank to the cabin. And a well-marked trail it had been, too. For a while Olive had wondered suspiciously if they were laying a trap of some kind.

Now this scene of confusion faintly disturbed him. Why had Cameron and the woman come here in the first place? And who had brought the sheriff's deputies? The chance that someone else, through blind luck, might beat him to the bounty nagged him with the persistence of an old wound.

He was forced to consider the possibility that the story of Doc Gafferty's death had spread from Starr by telegraph and special riders. Also, there was the deputy from whom he had taken the horse. Reason warned him that this would be a bad time for mingling with deputies.

Morning became afternoon. He waited for the deputies to go. The Texas sun shot fire arrows of light between the filigree leaves of mesquite. Finally a few of the lawmen made off toward the west, apparently under the impression that Cameron and the woman had struck for Mexico. That was good. Olive knew that Mexico, where he was thought to be a priest killer, would be the last place Cameron would make for.

Soon two more deputies rode west, and Olive was pleased to see them go. Get them out of the way. Lessen the chances of being robbed of his bounty. Two deputies remained behind, obviously under the impression that the old man and old woman had not told everything they knew.

Olive shifted impatiently, seeking an easier position for his shoulder. He cursed the wooden-headed stupidity of the deputies. With mingled hate and grim amusement, he watched the old woman, who had suddenly found her shrill, saw-toothed voice. She was upbraiding the old man for not killing Cameron and the Barringer woman when he had had the chance, an act which would have secured the reward money for them. Now it was too late. They would never have the chance again. Her voice carried on the air, like screams from a Comanche torture fire.

Olive did not envy the old man the few years of life that he had left to him. The old woman would never let him forget what his faintheartedness had cost them.

Now the last of the deputies tightened their cinches and rode west, as the others had done. Olive smiled to himself. By bits and pieces the picture had fitted together in his mind. Some-how—it didn't matter how—the old couple had captured the fugitives and had been on the verge of collecting the bounty. But the pair had escaped them—again, it didn't matter how. The thing that interested Olive was that the old man and his wife had lied to the deputies, sending them west when Olive knew that the pair probably had headed north, circling the Big Bend of the Bravo, making generally toward New Mexico.

But being reasonably sure was not good

enough now. Time had become a precious thing, a thread on which his life was hanging. He could not squander it on guesses and assumptions.

In the lacy shade of the mesquite he sat very still, waiting, watching, his feverish eyes missing nothing. The old couple and the overgrown boy were standing forlornly in their gravelly dooryard, watching the last of the deputies tip a rise and then gradually drop from sight. Suddenly the old man wheeled on the boy. There was a moment of furious talk and arm waving, then the boy headed down a long slope behind the cabin, toward a small brush corral where a black mule dozed in the sun.

Olive grinned. This was just what he had expected. The sudden excitement, the pleasure of his own cunning, worked on him like a drink of cold water. His brain seemed to clear itself of fever, even the throbbing in his shoulder became more bearable.

Legionnaire William Olive pulled himself to his feet. The war was not over, but he sensed that the final battle was now beginning.

In the brush corral Billy Bernson was hurriedly saddling the mule. The old man waited impatiently for his son to bring up the mule. His rifle stood in the corner of the cabin, but Cameron had taken all the shells so it was useless.

Mrs. Bernson, pitched uncertainly between sullen anger and last-chance hope, nagged compulsively and shrilly. Ike Bernson was no longer listening. His mind was methodically considering the more passable of the natural trails to the north. Soon he settled on a single passage, not a trail but a series of depressions and valleys that twisted through the Bexar. Part of an old Comanche war trail. It was the most natural and easiest way to cross the Bexar and get to New Mexico.

The old woman's shrill harangue stopped abruptly. She spoke quietly, with a stony calm. "Somebody comin'."

They both stood watching the big, wide-shouldered stranger coming toward them on the claybank.

"What you make of him?" Mrs. Bernson asked from the side of her small mouth.

" 'Nother deputy, I guess."

"Don't look like no deputy to me."

Nor to Ike, although he did not say so. There was something about this one that set him apart. A kind of brooding danger in the solid, punishing way he sat his saddle. Horses would not last long under a rider like this one.

"I don't like the looks of him," the old woman said.

Nor did Ike, but again he did not say so. "Might be one of the gun slingers the sheriff's hirin' nowadays, to help collect the taxes."

His wife shot him a cold glance that caused him to shrink. "I say he's a bounty hunter. He's got the look about him."

"We're all bounty hunters nowadays." But Ike knew what she meant. About this one there was something dark and purposeful.

When the rider came close enough they saw that he was smiling. Somehow Ike would have felt easier if he had been scowling or cursing. But he was smiling. And now they saw his eyes, which were glittery with fever. " 'Pears to be favorin' his nigh side," Ike said worriedly. "Maybe he's hurt."

"Or got the plague?" the old woman asked bitterly.

Ike sighed. He wished that he could signal Billy to hold off on saddling the mule. But the corral was down the grade and could not be seen from the house.

Something told Ike to go inside and get the old woman's scatter-gun. But there was something familiar about this stranger whom he had never seen before, and he couldn't say what it was. Could it be the way he dressed? Or his rig, or the faltering claybank?

A small light shone in a dark corner of Ike Bernson's mind. The outline of a memory was there, but he could not quite make it out.

The claybank plodded across the gravelly patch of dooryard and stopped in front of the cabin. The stranger looked at them, still smiling his heartless smile.

"What do you want?" the old woman asked sharply.

The rider lifted one hand and touched his flushed face. "Water first. Fresh water. Then talk."

"What kind of talk?" she demanded shrilly.

The stranger stared down at her with those glittery eyes. Her small, puckery mouth formed an angry "o." "Bounty hunter, ain't you?" she snapped.

"First the water," the rider said in his frosty tone.

Ike Bernson wiped a nervous hand across his mouth. "Get him some water," he said to his wife. When she didn't move, he raised his voice sharply. "Did you hear me, old woman?"

She blinked in surprise. Her husband's jaw was set at an angle of unusual stubbornness. Puzzled and vaguely worried, she backed her way into the cabin. With his right hand, the stranger drew a businesslike Spencer from the saddle boot, just on the chance that the old woman might have something other than water on her mind.

But she came back with a small granite dipper of water. Olive drank slowly, thoughtfully. The water tasted of stone and metal. At last he handed her his canteen. "Fill this."

The small mouth puckered peevishly. Ike

Bernson said harshly, "Do like he says!" And once again she backed into the cabin.

"Now," Olive said wearily, "on the other side of the rise there's a boy about to saddle a black mule. Get him back here to the cabin."

"How?" Ike asked. "I could holler, but he wouldn't hear, most likely."

"Just get him back," Olive told him. "Or I'll kill the old woman."

Bernson looked sharply at the stranger's eyes. All thoughts that this strange, hard-eyed rider might be bluffing were quickly dispelled. He stepped to the corner of the cabin and struck a heavy iron triangle several times. "Billy'll hear that and come. Now maybe you'll say what you want with him."

Olive shrugged with his good shoulder. "I don't want him at all. Just the mule."

The old woman came out of the cabin with the filled canteen. Olive took it, uncorked it, smelled of it, tasted it. The water was all right; she hadn't tried to poison him. He tied the canteen to the saddle horn. In a matter of seconds Billy Bernson appeared over the crest of the rise, loping the mule toward the cabin.

Billy reined up a short distance from the claybank and shot a hostile glance in Olive's direction. Then he looked at his father. "What's he want?"

"The mule," Ike Bernson said resignedly.

The youth laughed his high-pitched giggle. "That ain't likely. Me'n this black mule's got places to go."

"Get down," Ike said tonelessly, "or he'll kill your ma."

The boy glared all around in unfocused anger. "What is he?"

"Bounty hunter," the old woman snarled. "And a no-account one at that. Get down, like your pa says."

With what appeared to be sleepy indifference, Olive raised the rifle and aimed it at Billy's chest. "He'll get down," he said, with the chilly half-smile. "One way or another."

Billy stared wide-eyed into the Spencer's muzzle. He dismounted with no further objections.

"Now . . ." William Olive seemed to sigh. "Change saddles. From this horse of mine to the mule." He was much too weary to think of transferring his few belongings and the rifle boot to the mule. Easier to let Billy change entire rigs.

Ike Bernson said bitterly, "Judge you're a stranger in these parts. Do you know what the law says about horse stealin' hereabouts?"

Olive looked as if he might laugh, but didn't. He dismounted and sat on the porch step, looking at them out of a gray, unfeeling mask. Billy began to change saddles.

It was obvious to the Bernsons that the bounty

hunter was badly hurt. For a while Ike held some hope that the stranger would simply fall into unconsciousness.

But legionnaires were not often so obliging to their enemies. Olive merely sat and looked at them. After what seemed a long while he said, "I'm going to ask some questions. But first I'm going to tell you a story. About some Berbers I used to know."

He saw the blankness on their faces. "Guess you never met a Berber, did you? Well, they're fighters. First-class soldiers. And this is the way they interrogate prisoners. First, they get all the prisoners in a line, and the head man starts at the end of the line and asks the first prisoner a question. If the prisoner fails to answer fast enough to suit the head man, he's killed. Then and there. Usually they cut off his head. All in a matter of half a minute. Then the head man goes on to the second prisoner."

Olive studied their stiff-faced expressions. The Bernsons were getting the point of his story. He said, "Just like nothing at all had happened, the head man begins to question the second prisoner. He always gets his answers. I never knew a head man to have to question as many as three prisoners."

He smiled at them. The Bernsons were not comforted. Olive said, "Now, about the questions. I'll start with you." He indicated the old man.

"First of all, what were all the sheriff's deputies doing here this morning?"

Ike Bernson swallowed hard. "They was lookin' . . . lookin' for somebody."

"A paroled Confederate officer called Cameron?"

Ike hesitated only a second, then nodded.

"And a woman by the name of Barringer?"

Helplessly, the old man nodded again.

The "prisoners" stood frozen, even when Olive closed his eyes in thought. "Where did they go from here, Cameron and the Barringer woman?"

"They . . . they took an old Comanche war trail north, I think. That's just guessin', though."

"But you told the deputies they'd headed for Mexico."

Miserably the old man nodded. "These is hard times. There's reward money. I couldn't see givin' it up to a posse of deputies."

Olive smiled to himself. "How'd they come to be here in the first place?"

The old man told him about knowing Kate Barringer's husband before the war.

"The woman came to you for help," Olive thought aloud. "But she came alone. Did she and Cameron have a falling out?"

Ike Bernson shuffled uncomfortably. "I think she figured he'd stand a better chance without her."

Olive nodded to himself. No doubt about it; cut

free of the woman, Cameron would stand a fair chance of escaping. But it seemed that some men were born to self-destruction.

Olive rubbed his flushed face and added up what he had. Cameron and the woman were together again, that was the important thing. He asked, "How long since they got away from you?"

The old man spread his arms. "This mornin'. Little ahead of first light."

"What kind of shape were their horses in?"

Bernson was surprised that he didn't even bother to lie about the horses. "The woman's roan was pretty much done in. Couldn't tell about Cameron's animal—it run off."

Olive brightened. "They've got just the one horse between the two of them?"

"Unless Cameron caught the one he was ridin'."

Olive felt as if a heavy pack had been lifted from his back. He got to his feet. "You take my horse. I'll ride the mule. I want you to show me this trail you think they took."

Cameron lay on his back dragging huge gulps of air into his aching lungs. Ever since daylight they had been struggling across the craggy face of South Texas, Kate Barringer still riding the faltering roan, Cameron afoot. No telling where the dun was—probably in the hands of some Mexican bandit or outlaw deputy by this time.

How many miles had they come? Not as many as he had bloodying blisters on his feet. Of that he was quite certain.

He stared up at the savage sun. If they made it until sundown they might stand a chance. But he didn't really believe it.

He closed his eyes. In a little while he felt something cool and soothing on his forehead. Kate Barringer had dampened the tail of her petticoat and was sponging his face.

"How long have we been here?"

"Not long. Half an hour."

Worlds had crumbled in less time. He knew that they ought to be making for those vague, unreal mountains to the north, but he couldn't seem to make himself move.

"Is there any more water?"

She gave him her canteen and he sipped sparingly. After a while he said, "I don't understand it. Billy was supposed to return with the deputies around sunup. What happened to them? Where are they? Lord knows we left a trail that even our new brand of lawmen could follow. By rights they should have caught us hours ago."

"Maybe that's what the Bernsons were afraid of."

Cameron looked at her. "Yes . . ." It came as a long sigh. "That might be it. They could have sent the deputies chasing off to Mexico, or anywhere. That must mean that the old man and Billy still have their hearts set on the bounty money."

This thought did not disturb him. An old man, and a boy that was not very bright. He said, "If the Bernsons are behind us, maybe we ought to let them catch up." Somehow, the Bernsons would have rustled up some horses. And we're going to need horses, Cameron thought to himself. For he had no doubt that the real danger, William Olive, would not be far behind Ike and Billy.

They started again toward the mountains. With a little luck, Cameron was thinking, they would make the foothills and find a place to make a stand before nightfall. It might even be that they could lay an ambush for the Bernsons.

Cameron began to find a soft place in his heart for that boy and old man. In his exhaustion it was easy to dream, to shoulder reality to one side. He imagined that, when everything was finished, he would thank the Bernsons for taking such an interest in them. Soon Ike and Billy would be coming after them. On fresh horses. An old man and a dull-witted boy. At that moment it was all ridiculously simple in Cameron's mind. He and Kate Barringer would take the horses from Ike and Billy and make for New Mexico at top speed. They would leave Legionnaire Olive to eat dust and worry about his wounded shoulder.

Cameron stumbled alongside the roan,

clutching a stirrup leather for support. The sharp-edged gravel had worn through the soles of his boots. He had a suspicion that the bottoms of his feet had been shredded raw, but he preferred not to think about it right now. For a while the torture of broken blisters had almost taken his breath away, but it had been several hours since the pain had centralized itself. He stumbled on from knoll to knoll, from cactus to cactus, on what now felt to be wooden stumps. It was well that he had the Bernsons to think about.

"Captain!"

Cameron heard the word as if from a great distance. It was Kate Barringer, but he couldn't make out where the voice was coming from. He stared with the furious concentration of a Sioux shaman but saw only a kind of turbulent darkness. He smelled earth and stone. His mouth was gritty. He realized that he had fallen straight forward, on his face. His mouth was full of gravel.

Kate? But he only thought the word in his mind. He tried to move, to lift his face out of the gravel. He wouldn't have believed that such a small thing could have been so difficult. Now there were firm hands on his shoulders. Kate was turning him over.

"Captain, are you all right?"

It irritated him that she continued to call him "Captain." He was not a captain. He was a fugitive with a price on his head. But he had a name. Wardson Lee Cameron. But this was also in his mind, not spoken. He spat out some of the gravel.

"You're almost dead with exhaustion," she said, holding the canteen to his mouth. He rinsed his mouth. Then he took a swallow of the water and rested. He stared into the blue, endless sky. She said, "We'll have to stop here."

"Can't stop. Until we find a place."

"What kind of place?"

Cameron tried to think like a cavalryman behind enemy lines, looking for just the right place to set an ambush. "A place of high ground, a stream, a box canyon, something like that."

"There's nothing like that, just a little knoll up ahead."

Cameron raised his head and looked at the flat wasteland. The knoll was just that, not enough elevation to be called a hill. It afforded very little in the way of cover, being stark naked except for prickly pear and a few rocks. A poor place to set an ambush.

"It'll have to do," he sighed. He looked at the roan. The animal stood head down, legs spraddled, eyes dull. Kate Barringer had been walking since the last stop, in the hope of saving the horse. Now they were all played out. Like it or not, this was the end of the road.

ELEVEN

Ike Bernson had been thinking. A thousand dollars—eleven hundred, including the bounty on the woman—was a lot of money. It didn't seem right that this hard-eyed stranger should get all of it. After all, it had been the Bernsons who had captured the fugitives in the first place.

"Way I look at it," the old man suddenly blurted, "you're twelve hours closer to that bounty money than you would of been if you hadn't come to our place. On top of that, I'm showin' you the trail. And I sent them deputies chasin' theirselves off towards Mexico. All that ought to be worth somethin', wouldn't you say?"

Olive looked at him with eyes that were swimming with fever. "We'll see. You haven't found the trail yet. So far, all I've seen is the tracks left by the deputies."

"I'll show it to you. Jobs like this take a little time."

Olive studied him narrowly. The old man thought he could hold back all useful information until he had nailed down a part of the bounty. The old fool. He didn't know that he was lucky just to be alive.

But Olive sighed resignedly. "I've been on

the trail a long time. I've earned the bounty."

"Sure, sure!" Ike said excitedly. He was beginning to smell money. "But think how much tougher it would be if I didn't pitch in and help. A stranger could blunder around this prairie a week without findin' a trace. And mister, you don't look any too pert to me, if you want the straight of it."

He was digging his own grave with words and greed. But Legionnaire Olive had long since given up any thought of saving fools from their own folly. "All right," he said meekly. "How much?"

The black mule had a hard, stiff-legged gait that kept Olive's shoulder continually ablaze with pain. But the claybank was beginning to stagger, even under the frail weight of the old man. So it didn't really matter now what he said or did—the old man's usefulness was almost over as far as Olive was concerned.

Ike didn't see it that way. The whirring inside his head could almost be heard as he created cunning little treacheries. He was gleeful that the stranger had been so easy to convince. Maybe, just maybe, old Ike Bernson would wind up with the whole bounty after all.

"Well," he said, eyeing Olive shrewdly, "seein' as how they's three of us, me'n Billy'n the old woman . . . don't seem no more'n fair that we get half the reward."

Olive could almost have pitied the old man if there had been any pity in him. Ike Bernson was dead; he just didn't realize it yet. Olive didn't see that it could do any harm, making promises to a dead man. "Half of everything sounds a little stiff to me." No sense appearing *too* eager to give away five hundred and fifty American dollars.

"But think what we done!" Ike said, his small eyes glinting with delight. "All the time we saved you. Gettin' rid of the deputies. Think about it!"

Olive pretended to think about it. All he could actually think about was the pain that was tearing through him. But he pretended. "All right," he said at last, and exhaustion and sickness made it sound sincere. "Half. Looks like I've got no choice."

Ike Bernson could hardly keep from cackling his glee. Half was much more than he had hoped for.

But greed is a worm that keeps on growing and is never truly satisfied. It wasn't long before the old man began thinking about the whole bounty and how he could get it. But he was cautious, as well as greedy. This stranger was sick, plenty sick, but still dangerous. Besides, he might need Olive's help when it came to actually capturing the fugitives. No sense hurrying when everything was going so nicely.

Olive knew what the old man was thinking. He didn't care. Let the old fool plan and scheme to his heart's content. It might well be the last pleasure he would ever know.

They continued to the north. Olive had rarely hated a living thing as savagely as he hated that hard-gaited mule, but he knew that the claybank wouldn't last a mile under stonelike weight. He rode on, wrapped in shimmering pain.

"Ah!" Ike Bernson exclaimed in a tone of extreme self-satisfaction. "What'd I tell you? This is where they came out of the bottom, strikin' north."

Olive shook himself free of an almost overpowering lethargy. "Where?"

The old man pointed out the tracks that straggled out of Turkey River's sandy bottom. The tracks of one horse, and one man afoot. A long sigh of satisfaction whistled between Olive's teeth. He had been smart to bring the old man along. "Where are they making for?"

"Can't say. Neither can they, if I'm any judge. Just follerin' that old war trail out across the Bexar, like I figgered."

That was good enough for Olive. A man desperate, as Cameron must be, did not need a particular reason for taking a certain road; he simply took the way that seemed easiest and fastest. "What lies ahead of us on this trail?"

Ike Bernson shrugged. "Nothin' much. Gravel and needle grass and thickets of prickly pear."

Olive was thinking with a soldier's brain, the

way that he knew Cameron would be thinking. A man afoot wasn't going to get far in this barren flatland; his only chance was to hold up somewhere and try an ambush. He asked the old man about places where Cameron might lay a trap for them.

Ike shook his head. "Nothin' out there but flats, like you see. Turkey River's the only water hereabouts, and it runs dry most of the year."

Ordinarily Olive would have taken it easy. No need to take chances. Keep the pressure on for perhaps another day and Cameron would have come to the end of his string.

But this was not an ordinary situation. Olive could feel his fever mounting, his skin becoming hotter and drier.

No, he could not rely on time as an ally. He must close with the enemy as soon as possible, before he became weaker and the enemy stronger.

They rode to the north, following the tracks of the horse and the man. They stopped for a moment at the place where Cameron had fallen. The prints of the roan's forehooves were wide apart where he had been halted, telling Olive that the animal was as exhausted as the man and the woman.

Olive urged the mule forward at a quicker gait. He lifted his head and sniffed the air like a wild Arab dog catching the scent of fresh blood.

For a long while the old man had been watching

223

Olive with growing interest. Ike had also considered the element of time. It was running with Ike and against Olive. He could see that Olive had decided to catch Cameron and have it out as soon as possible.

Ike would have liked to take his time. Lie back out of reach, let the sun and the desert do its work. Then move in for an easy kill. Ike thought about the bounty. More and more the thought of splitting it with Olive galled him. He soon began to think of ways to avoid it.

Olive held to the saddle horn with both hands. Ike studied the gray, sweatless face and said, "You ain't lookin' none too good to me, mister. What say we spell the animals awhile? That bounty ain't goin' to get away from us."

Olive regarded him bleakly. All right, he thought. It's up to you, old man. He nodded. "For a little while. Not long. Cameron and the woman can't be far ahead."

The old man beamed.

They reined up in a wasteland of prickly pear and coarse sand. Ike Bernson was the model of a helpful companion and concerned partner. He helped Olive down from the saddle. He staked the claybank and the mule. His eyes slightly glazed, Olive lay down in the shade of the mule. The old man chattered like a midwife.

"Here, take a swig of this." He held a canteen to Olive's mouth and Olive drank. "Now just lay back and take her easy. Shut your eyes. A few minutes one way or 'nother won't make any difference."

Obediently, Olive closed his eyes. He could read the old man's thoughts even with his eyes shut. He could almost see Ike grinning down at him. The rich Ike Bernson. The proud new owner of eleven hundred American dollars. Almost.

Olive's craving for rest was a treacherous thing. The ground seemed soft as he stretched out on it; his hard body was soothed and comforted by it. Almost without knowing it, he found himself drifting toward darkness.

Legionnaire Olive brought himself to with alarm. His feverish skin prickled with the effort to sweat. He peered up at the sky through slitted lids. He turned his head slightly; Ike Bernson was not to be seen. Olive turned his head a bit more.

He relaxed. There was the old man, just where Olive had known he would be. Very carefully and very quietly, Ike was drawing the Spencer out of the saddle boot.

Just as the muzzle cleared the boot, the old man died. Olive had despised him for his niggling greed, but he had not hated him otherwise. He felt no desire to make him suffer. All in all, Olive felt, Ike Bernson might consider himself lucky. Certainly there were many harder ways to die than taking a knife quickly through the heart.

The old man gave a little grunt of surprise. That was all. He died without another sound. There was some mindless kicking, of course, but this was mere muscular reflex. It always happened in such cases. Taken all together, Olive was rather pleased with the job.

He grabbed the mule by the bit before the animal got a chance to smell the blood. Then he dusted the rifle and put it back into the boot. With an effort that left him panting, he climbed back into the saddle.

Without a thought for the claybank, he left the animal staked where it was sure to die slowly of thirst. He didn't look back at the still body of the old man. Picking up the tracks, he kneed the mule along the old trail that Comanches had once followed to war in Mexico.

The sun was still more than an hour high when Olive raised the knoll where he knew the enemy waited. He preferred to think of Cameron as the enemy. It seemed more orderly, more soldierly. He thought of the knoll as an outpost to be taken. His thoughts fell naturally into military patterns.

He couldn't say exactly how he knew that this knoll was the place. An old soldier got to know these things. Cameron and the woman were there somewhere, just below the crest of the rise, most likely, the played-out roan staked a little farther back. He smiled faintly to himself. How often in the past he had risked his life on such scraps of unprovable knowledge!

He studied the terrain before him with professional coolness. As a battlefield for massed armies, it would have been magnificent; as a field for savage little outpost skirmishes, it was merely suicidal. For all concerned.

Again, the ideal procedure would be to wait and let time do your work for you. But time was growing precious and was not to be squandered.

Olive got down from the mule and unsheathed the Spencer. The earth seemed to tilt beneath his feet. He stumbled, almost fell. He stood for a moment, panting. Then he tied the mule to a thornbush and took the canteen and the extra ammunition from the saddle pocket. Finally he turned and studied the knoll and the monotonous and deadly flatland that surrounded it.

Well, he thought, I've fought in worse places. But not often. Yet it was comforting, in a way, to know that worse places did exist and that he had survived them.

Olive sat on the ground in order to get a better perspective of the land that lay between himself and the knoll. No land was perfectly flat. Even those great Algerian oceans of sand, the Grand Erg and the Iguidi, rippled and undulated and, on meticulous inspection, afforded here and there small depressions in which the experienced soldier might find life-preserving cover.

Legionnaire Olive studiously discovered and catalogued such places here. In his mind he mapped his route to the knoll. It was all rather simple when one blocked out the unessentials. The orders were to carry the objective, at all costs. In the Legion all orders were expected to be carried out promptly, efficiently, and "at all costs."

On attacking the knoll, Olive could have wished for covering fire. But such luxuries were not often the lot of a legionnaire. Neither did the military maxim which held that an attacking force should be twice the strength of the defending force apply to the Legion. Legionnaires were destined for untimely death. And anyway, it rarely mattered if an objective was taken or a battle won. The causes for which the Legion fought were inevitably lost to begin with.

Olive stayed there for almost half an hour. He had been staring fixedly at the knoll, but his mind had been in places like Ourgla, El Golea, Tamanrasset, places with the sound of poetry and death. And Camerone—no legionnaire ever again would forget Camerone.

Perhaps it was the similarity of names that dragged Olive's attention back to Cameron. He pulled himself to his feet and ran toward the first of a dozen small depressions that he had mapped out in his mind. He ran with a lunging, one-sided gait and fell gasping for breath into the hollow of earth. Due to Legion training he fell on his rifle, sighting along the barrel on the chance that the enemy might show himself.

But, of course, the enemy would not open fire so early. The Berber was usually armed with poorly-made Belgian muskets. He wisely waited until the attacker was quite close before opening fire.

Olive gathered his strength, rose to his knees, and ran toward the next depression. He was shocked and incredulous when a heavy bullet struck the ground only inches from his left foot. How could that be? An Arab would not open fire so soon. And he was almost never armed with a rifle.

Olive fell into the slight hollow of earth. His shoulder blazed, his heart beat wildly. He lay gasping for air, trying to figure out what had happened.

Of course. His mind must have wandered. He was not in Algeria. He was not even in the Legion. And the enemy behind that miserable rocky knoll was not a Berber tribesman but an ex-Confederate officer by the name of Cameron.

The hard-textured sea of gravel shimmered and trembled. Olive rubbed his eyes. This fever, his inability to collect and focus his thoughts, was beginning to worry him. Perhaps he was sicker than he had believed.

Well, there were no doctors on the battle line.

No hope for medical attention until the battle was over. This was something a legionnaire learned to accept. He might lie watching his life pumping hot and red into the desert sand. No medical attention until the battle was over.

He raised his head, and a second bullet screamed past him. This was not a good place. There was not enough protection here. On the map in his mind he studied the third depression. It was deeper than this one, besides which there was some concealing prickly pear. He got to his feet and lunged toward it.

Something tugged lightly at his left sleeve. The iron discipline of the Legion did not allow him to notice it. He stumbled on to the third station and fell on his rifle. This time he fired just as the gray crown of a hat was disappearing behind the knoll.

A small geyser of sand and gravel spurted up inches from where the hat had been. Olive grinned. That would give the bloody Berber something to think about.

Now, in the moment of quiet, he looked at his sleeve. From around a tear a sick, dark blood was welling up. But the pain, if any existed, was consumed in the fire of the old infected wound. With professional indifference Olive observed the flow of blood for a moment. Then he forgot it. A scratch. Soldiers of the Legion did not concern themselves with scratches.

He lay back and regarded the endless depth of sky. Here in his shallow, gravel-like depression, he began to realize that he would not come out of this fight alive. Even if he carried the knoll and killed Cameron and the woman. Death perched on his burning shoulder like a sharp-taloned bird. He had had this feeling before but never this strong.

He gulped air and considered his position. *La Légion* trained its soldiers well. He had never truly stopped believing in "*A moi la Légion*" or that his destiny was death. He had merely slipped for a little while into a childish dream. When he killed Sergent-Chef Ciano he had thought that he had killed his past. But that was not so. One day, perhaps, the Legion would die, but a legionnaire would not kill it.

It puzzled him that a man-created thing like the Legion could be hated and revered at the same time. He sensed its mystique but could not explain it. Blood shed in battle was stronger than life itself. He sensed that now. The Legion had known it from the beginning.

Olive sighed, turned in his shallow grave, and again regarded the knoll. Here he was, and there the enemy was. That was what it boiled down to, not bounty money. He would not know what to do with money if he had it.

Guns and knives. He knew what to do with them.

TWELVE

Kate Barringer was the first to see Olive coming toward them on the black mule. She made a little sound of alarm. Cameron peered over the lip of the knoll and knew that this was where they would decide on who would live and who would die.

"I wonder what happened to the Bernsons," Kate said after a drawn-out silence.

Cameron didn't answer. They watched the slumped figure, riding with the weight of stone, coming toward them. Cameron rested the barrel of the Henry on a bit of outcrop and waited for Olive to come within range.

Olive reined the mule to a stop. They watched him dismount and draw his rifle.

Kate looked sharply at Cameron. "How can he know we're here?"

Cameron shrugged. He understood Olive's thinking, but it was not an easy thing to explain. He watched Olive sling the canteen, turn, and look directly at the knoll. Cameron scowled. Was this ex-legionnaire thinking of making a one-man frontal attack on his position? True, the knoll would have been no good in a routine skirmish, but in a man-against-man fight it was an enormous advantage. Olive, an experienced soldier, must know that.

Cameron couldn't know that Olive's mind, at that moment, was deep in the sand ocean of the Iguidi. The way Olive stood there beside the mule, a stonelike figure of confidence and determination, made Cameron's skin prickle. Was it possible that Olive knew something that Cameron didn't know? Had this former soldier of France marshaled reinforcements from somewhere? Was Olive himself merely setting a trap, using himself as diversionary bait?

Cameron turned and searched those great open spaces on his flanks and rear. No, that sort of trickery was not possible, not in a place like this.

When Olive sat on the ground, facing the knoll, Cameron understood that he was systematically examining the ground that separated their two positions. So he had no reinforcements.

Olive sat motionless. Ten, fifteen minutes passed. Kate Barringer asked worriedly, "What is he doing?"

"I think he's getting ready to attack."

Even Kate could see that a frontal attack would be suicidal. "How can he?"

Cameron grunted. He was beginning to understand some of it, a little of it.

Kate asked, "Tonight?"

"I don't think he'll wait that long." He had

seen Olive sway unsteadily when he dismounted.

Kate didn't understand. "He knows you have a rifle. He would be crazy to attack in full light."

"That's about what it amounts to. He probably didn't give his shoulder a chance to heal. I wouldn't be surprised if he had gangrene by this time."

For several minutes they said nothing. And still Olive sat, like some hunched, ferocious rock. Cameron watched him over the sights of the Henry, but the range was too great for the weapon. "I don't think he'll attack," Kate said at last. "Not until it's dark."

"He'll attack," Cameron said.

Now they saw Olive getting slowly to his feet. He started toward the knoll, running awkwardly, the way a drunk or wounded man would run. Cameron let him come. When the legionnaire came within range, Cameron squeezed the trigger.

The rifle bellowed. Cameron saw where the bullet struck the ground. Olive lunged to one side, came on a few steps, and dived into a shallow depression, possibly an old buffalo wallow. At a thousand yards the Henry was shooting about two feet to the left. Cameron made the necessary adjustment and waited for Olive to make his next move.

Cautiously, Olive raised his head above the lip of the depression. Cameron fired again and the head quickly disappeared. Kate Barringer asked tautly, "Is he . . . ?"

"No, the bullet went high."

Frowning, Cameron jacked another brass cartridge into the Henry. His second shot had been a distinct miss. The fault, he knew, was not with the rifle. It was with himself.

Kate was looking at him in a strange way. "Is something wrong?"

"No." But he smiled wryly to himself. The flamboyant gallantry of Manassas had no longer been apparent at Vicksburg. And yet the phrase, "valiant enemy," was not as laughable as it would be in a later, more worldly, time.

Valiant, of course, was not the word for Legionnaire William Olive. But he had courage, and this was something that Cameron could admire. Now Cameron was wondering if all this had something to do with the bullet passing harmlessly over his target's head.

He couldn't be sure. But he could be sure of one thing—a soldier of the Legion would be harboring no such dangerous doubts in *his* mind.

Olive was continuing his lunging race toward the knoll. Cameron set himself to fire when the legionnaire seemed to disappear, like a prairie dog, into the ground. Almost immediately a violent geyser of powdered rock exploded beside Cameron's head. The prairie dog was firing back—and Cameron was glad. From now on it would not be so much like putting bullets into a corpse.

Olive reappeared, a gray-faced ghost out of an open grave.

Cameron aimed carefully, taking his time. Olive ran clumsily, zig-zagging across the open expanse of gravel.

Cameron fired.

Incredibly, Olive did not go down. He stumbled, caught up his gait, and raced on with what appeared to be growing strength. Once again the legionnaire disappeared. The muzzle of the Spencer showed over the lip of the wallow. Three bullets tore through the top of Cameron's makeshift breastworks. A slashing hail of gravel blinded him. He lunged at Kate Barringer, knocking her away from the crest of the knoll.

He couldn't see. Dirt and stinging tears filled his eyes. He could feel the blood from the dozen small gravel wounds in his face, but he could not see. He rubbed his eyes frantically. It did no good. He fumbled with the rifle. Kate was shouting urgently into his ears. What she was saying did not register in his brain.

Somewhere in the blur of light and shadow he could almost hear Olive's laughter and see his wolfish grin. Dying is easier when you take an enemy with you. Any old soldier would tell you that. Crazy thoughts sped in and out of Cameron's mind. His sight was returning. But not fast

236

enough. Olive would be up that gentle slope and over the lip of the knoll before Cameron could distinguish one blurred shape from another. . . .

In some blocked-off corner of his mind Cameron heard a faint but distinctive sound. Metal on metal. The hard snapping sound of hammer driving futilely against firing pin. Dirt in the Spencer's action. A man dying of gangrene did not remember to check such things.

The knowledge that Olive's rifle was inoperative should have sent Cameron's hope soaring. He experienced no such sensation. Olive would have a knife and he recalled the death of the priest. Besides that, Olive might be armed with a revolver for all Cameron knew.

Kate Barringer cried out urgently, "Captain, give me the rifle!" She had said it several times before, but he had not heard her. Now it was too late. A shape loomed suddenly into Cameron's blurred vision. A shadow of a shadow, as seen at the bottom of a murky pool. And the cold glint of a dying sun as it struck metal.

Cameron fired into that sudden flash of light on knife-steel.

It seemed that a long time passed, but the sun still had a few minutes to go when Cameron began to see normally again. Kate Barringer dribbled water from the canteen into his reddened eyes. Cameron blinked the water away and looked at

Kate's face. It was dirty and streaked and lined with exhaustion. Cameron was surprised to realize that he liked it.

"Can you see?"

He nodded.

They did not do much talking. After a while he went to Olive's body and looked at it without emotion. Olive had been a soldier, and he had died with the heat of the battle in his blood, not slowly and coldly, with only the stench of gangrene in his nostrils.

Cameron was weak with fatigue, but not too weak to cover the body with rocks to keep the coyotes away. While he did that, Kate untied the mule and brought it in. She gave the two animals half the water in the canteens.

Cameron inspected the roan. With rest and care the two animals ought to get them to New Mexico and safety.

Night came silently to the prairie. Cameron and Kate Barringer took the horses away from the knoll, away from the body. They threw their blankets beneath a twisted mesquite tree and let the horses eat what they would of the yellowish leaves. Every bone in Cameron's body ached. His feet were raw and swollen. A colony of sand lice nested in his beard and hair.

He was feverish with fatigue, and yet he could not sleep. Tomorrow, with luck, they would make it to the great plateau, across the Bexar, then across the Llano Estacado, and finally to the territories. With luck.

He looked at Kate Barringer. She seemed to be asleep. But after a while she said, "I'm sorry."

"About what?"

"The Bernsons. A lot of things. You could have been to New Mexico now if it hadn't been for me."

"Olive would have handed me over to the scalawag police if it hadn't been for you."

She was silent for several minutes, searching for the right words. Then, "If you don't mind, I'll stay with you until we get out of Texas. If we get out."

Cameron looked at her. "I don't mind."

"I won't bother you any more, once we're away."

"Is that what you want?"

". . . I didn't say that."

He was too tired to wonder exactly what his feelings were in relation to Kate Barringer. She had saved his life. They had been together for what seemed like a long time. And they got along. He hadn't had time to think beyond that.

"Why don't we talk about it later?" he said.

". . . All right."

More minutes of silence passed. Kate had fallen asleep. In some unexplainable way, Cameron's taut muscles began to relax. He felt as though he had just solved a nagging problem—but he wasn't sure what the problem had been.

No matter. He began to relax. And then he slept.

Center Point Large Print
600 Brooks Road / PO Box 1
Thorndike, ME 04986-0001 USA

(207) 568-3717

US & Canada:
1 800 929-9108
www.centerpointlargeprint.com